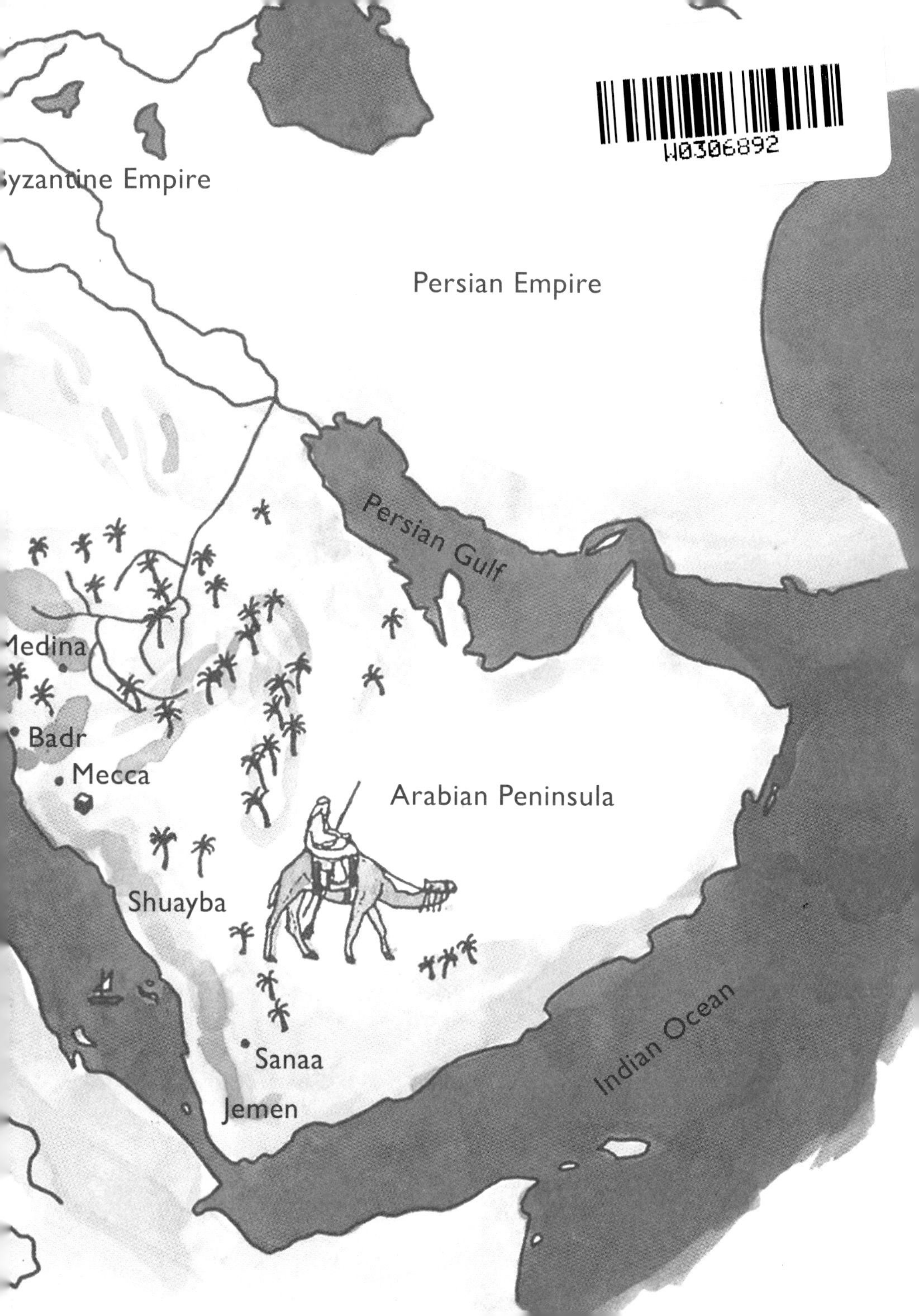

yzantine Empire
Persian Empire
Persian Gulf
Medina
Badr
Mecca
Arabian Peninsula
Shuayba
Sanaa
Jemen
Indian Ocean

Muhammad ﷺ and the Call of Heaven

The Life of the Prophet

Told by Andrea Faridah Busemann
Illustrated by Fatima Aksoy
Translated by Sheila Khalaf-Decker
English text revised by Lesley Alzaka

Muhammad ﷺ and the Call of Heaven

The Life of the Prophet

Told by Andrea Faridah Busemann
Illustrated by Fatima Aksoy
Translated by Sheila Khalaf-Decker
English text revised by Lesley Alzaka

VIBE – International Islamic Education Publishing House

بسم الله الرحمن الرحيم

Original German title: Muhammad und der Ruf des Himmels

Illustrations: Fatima Aksoy
Cover design and typesetting: Grafikdesign Holzapfel
Printed in the EU
First Edition (German) 2010
ISBN 978-3-939808-12-1
www.vibe-online.de

For my family

Preface

Al-hamdulillah,

All praise and thanks be to Allah that after many years of intensive work this book can finally be released.

It was a challenge never met before to take up the classical Islamic tradition of the prophetic biography[1] and to give it a literary form to be readily understood by children and young people in the language of our time. The idea was to relate the events in an enthralling and lively way without distorting them in the process.

Faridah Busemann is able to see things from the perspective of the historical persons, immersing herself in their world. It is from these perspectives that the author depicts the events, always abiding by traditional legacy.

In keeping with Islamic tradition according to which Prophet Muhammad and other great personalities in Islam are not pictured, Fatima Aksoy illustrated this book with a lot of delicacy and care, making every effort to stay true to the original historical circumstances.

Our particular thanks go to those who have played their part in rechecking the sources and revising the text. If, in spite of all care and attention, there should be any errors in the text, we will gladly receive any feedback and comments. May Allah forgive us and bless all those who read this story of Muhammad's life.

The publishers

1) The primary sources used to write this book were the Sira of Ibn Ishaq entitled "The Life of Muhammad" as well as Martin Ling's biography of the Prophet, entitled "Muhammad: His Life Based on the Earliest Sources". Both books have been published in German by Spohr Publishers.

Table of Contents

Halima

The Year of the Great Drought

Halima narrowed her eyes to slits. In the distance she could see the blurred outlines of a city. "At last!" she sighed. With the corner of her sleeve she wiped the sweat off her forehead. The heat had become insufferable. Never in her life had Halima experienced a drought like this year. Her legs were aching and she was so exhausted she could hardly sit upright on her jenny. Even the little donkey, who was usually really playful, could hardly take any more. With great effort she set her hooves on the blazing hot stones, the ground was parched and the yellow twigs of dried bushes were rustling softly in the wind. The few waterholes in the desert had run dry or become mere trickles; the udders of the milk goats were empty. Whenever people stepped out of their houses or tents, they looked up at the sky in sorrow, but not the slightest bit of cloud was there to dim the glistening blue sky. Halima had put a pebble in her mouth and now playfully moved it back and forth with her tongue. She did that sometimes when she got too thirsty, because the smooth, cool stone made her feel refreshed for a few moments. Halima's gaze wandered to her husband Harith, who had dismounted and was leading his camel along by its reins. He was patiently striding beside the animal, but Halima knew the heat was getting to him as well.

If only they would arrive soon, especially for the sake of the baby! Halima was holding her son, covering him with a cloth to protect him from the scorching sun. Almost the whole length of the journey the little boy had been weeping and whining. Halima was no longer able to satisfy his thirst. Meanwhile she was feeling dried up just like the sweet brown dates she usually loved to eat.

In Mecca, the city they were finally approaching now, they would soon get water and a skin of milk, and what was just as important: with a bit of luck they would also find a foster child. For this was the actual reason of their journey.

Like all nomads, Harith and Halima led a simple and austere life without any wealth. But on the other hand, they felt free and independent. Halima had often watched the men of her tribe dashing across the sandy plains on their galloping camels, their faces aglow with excitement. With coarse voices they sang the songs of the desert. Proud and brave is what they were.

Sitting around their campfires at night, the women and men of the tribe told each other stories of love and war, wisdom and adventures, surpassing each other with their words, as expressive and beautiful as poetry.

Halima knew that the Meccans from the Tribe of Quraysh secretly admired her people. They wished for their own offspring to be endowed with the qualities of the nomads. Besides, children who grew up in the desert fell ill less often. Therefore many families in Mecca had a particular custom: soon after a son was born, they gave him to the nomadic tribes in the desert. Life in the barren lands made the children strong and sharpened their minds, and only after a couple of years did they return to their parents in the city.

Even the Banu Saad, as the tribe was called that Halima belonged to, regularly took in children. In compensation, their parents sent the Banu Saad provisions such as spices or raisins or other things they could not normally obtain. The richer the foster children's families were, the better the reward that could be expected in return. Halima was hoping for such a relationship. The city of Mecca gradually became silhouetted against the dark and rocky range of hills, when Halima noticed her husband Harith turning around towards her. "Hold on", his eyes said, "we have almost made it."

Mecca

Looking for a Foster Child

The city of Mecca was situated in a wide and stony valley, surrounded by rocky brown mountains. The plains were the place where the paths of great trade caravans crossed. They carried goods from Syria via Mecca to Yemen or to the kingdom of Abyssinia and vice versa. Thus Mecca grew into a popular centre of trade. Towards evening, when the searing sun started to set, the city came to life.

Merchants and buyers met in the alleys and at the market in order to do business, replenish their supplies and exchange news. Trade goods of all kinds were offered for sale and sold with a lot of haggling.

Pack camels carried bulging bags that were filled with fragrant spices. Colourful bales of cloth were unloaded as well as crates and boxes filled with incense, perfume and other merchandise.

Vendors at their stalls cried their wares such as dates and figs. On the ground, pots and bowls stood stacked, waiting to be sold. Jewellery

and daggers, decorated with silver, changed hands. "Do come closer," the merchants called. "All our goods are of the best quality!"
Anyone who was thirsty could have his cup filled with water or goat's milk. This opportunity was taken by the many pilgrims who came pouring to Mecca from all parts of the earth. They all were on their way to the Kaaba, the great shrine of the city. The cube-shaped building was already very old; Prophet Ibrahim and his son Ismail had built it as a house of prayer, for worshipping the one great God.

Many centuries had since gone by. God, who was called "Allah" by the people in Arabia, had more and more passed into oblivion as time went on.
Instead, idols made of wood and stone had been set up in the holy house. The pilgrims who now came and entered the Kaaba believed that these idols possessed special powers. Therefore they laid foods at their feet or threw coins in a basin at the Kaaba. As a reward for these offerings they hoped for many children, a rich harvest or other things.
Halima did not believe in this kind of idolatry. She knew that the custodians of the Kaaba collected all the offerings every night to put them into their own pockets.
The young woman pushed her way through the thick crowd. For hours on end she had been looking for a suitable foster child, but to no avail so far. She gradually began to doubt that the decision to go to Mecca had been right. She had seen a few boys she would have liked, but each time their parents had chosen another foster family. There was only one baby left that had not yet been turned over to a foster mother. The father had died on a journey before this boy had been born, and his mother, Amina, was almost as poor as Halima herself. She sighed. Not much could be expected from such a relationship, taking the boy in would hardly be worthwhile.
Disappointed, Halima and her husband decided to leave the city again, but when they were about to set off, Halima hesitated. On a sudden impulse, she said to her husband: "Let me at least have a

look at the boy. I don't want to be the only one among my friends who comes back without a foster child." "As you like," her husband answered in astonishment. This was probably not going to be a good deal, but Harith was willing to leave the decision in this matter to his wife. "We might receive a blessing for taking the boy with us," he thought.

Abdul Muttalib, the little boy's grandfather, had almost given up hope that he would find a foster mother for his grandson.

All the greater was his joy when shortly afterwards he met a young woman from the tribe of Banu Saad, who was willing to take in the child.

"What is your name?" Abdul Muttalib asked the young woman. "Halima Saadiya," she answered.

"Halima Saadiya – the gentle and fortunate one," Abdul Muttalib replied with a smile. "A wonderful name!"

In Abdul Muttalib's house, Halima was kindly welcomed by his daughter-in-law, Amina, the child's mother.
Full of expectation, Halima moved closer to the soft bed made of furs and cloth in which the baby was lying. At once Halima sensed the particular atmosphere that surrounded the child. There was a unique radiance on the boy's face. In this instant, she knew it had been right to come back. Halima cautiously lifted the boy up and took him in her arms. From the first moment she loved the boy like her own son. His name was Muhammad ﷺ, the Praised One.

The Desert

An Uncanny Encounter

There was hardly an area that was drier and more arid than the area of the Banu Saad. In this part of the desert, water was more precious than gold. Time after time there were periods where food and water supplies became dangerously scarce. People and animals alike were suffering from hunger and thirst. Several times Harith and Halima had also gone through such times of hardship, but ever since little Muhammad ﷺ came to live with them, their lives had changed. It was indeed a miracle: The goats found enough greens to eat and their udders were full. The water skins that were tied to the camel saddles were filled and every evening there was a pleasant smell of cooked food wafting around the tent.

Halima's own son, Abdullah, and little Muhammad ﷺ grew up like brothers. Together they explored their surroundings and played with the goats.

One day, however, Abdullah returned to the tent camp alone, he was running as fast as he could. His breath was ragged and his heart was pounding with anxiety. "Mother! Father!" he called, "There were two strangers dressed in white garments! They knocked my brother from the tribe of Quraysh to the ground and plunged their hands into his chest!" Scared to death, Harith and Halima dropped everything and rushed off.

Soon they saw Muhammad ﷺ standing between the goats, pale but upright. "What happened?" Halima asked him, worriedly. "Suddenly two men appeared", Muhammad ﷺ replied. "They laid me on the ground, then they opened my chest with their hands and searched for something inside!" With a frown Harith looked around in all directions, but there was no trace of the two men. There was not even a footprint left in the sand.

Halima pulled Muhammad ﷺ towards her. Cautiously she examined him for signs of an injury. But all she discovered was a somewhat strange-looking mark on his skin between his shoulder blades, which seemed not to be a cause for concern.

Halima sighed with relief, but she was shaken to the very core. When she looked at her husband, she realised that he felt the same way. Harith's face still looked concerned and thoughtful. In the evening, when the two children were asleep, he said to Halima, "I have been thinking. Maybe those were evil spirits who wanted to take possession of him. It all seems sinister to me. In the end, we might be held accountable if something happens to the boy. I think we should take him back to his mother."

"You are right," Halima answered sadly, "maybe he will be safer there." Releasing her foster child did not come easy to Halima. She had taken him in her heart like her own son. Abdullah would be devastated, too. He was attached to Muhammad ﷺ like to a real brother. Besides, Halima was concerned about their future. Never before had they fared as well as they had in the past few months. It was as if all their wishes had come true since they had taken the boy in. "What is to become of us when Muhammad no longer lives with us?" she wondered. "Will we still be well provided for, or will we soon suffer from hunger and thirst again?"

And what was Amina, Muhammad's mother, going to say on this matter? "Hopefully she is not going to reproach us," Halima sighed. With a heavy heart, Halima and Harith set out for Mecca with little Muhammad ﷺ. They would have loved so much to keep him with them longer, but they sensed that a different path was predestined for Muhammad ﷺ.

Amina

A Severe Stroke of Fate

Amina heard a knock on her door.

When a few moments later she opened the door, she saw her son standing in front of her, accompanied by his foster parents. Full of surprise she embraced her boy. How he had grown since she had last seen him and how strong he had become!

"Welcome to my home!" Amina called happily, when they had exchanged their greetings and entered the house.

"You must all be exhausted from the long journey," Amina said. "Please do sit down. I will fetch something to drink."

After they had rested for a while, Harith and Halima began to explain why they had come so suddenly. Hesitantly, they gave an account of the eerie incident in the desert. "It was so strange," they said, "These men did not leave any traces. Without a doubt they were jinn."

Amina looked at her visitors' worried faces, but she saw no reason to reproach the foster parents for what had happened to her son.

Quite the contrary – Amina knew that Halima and Harith had always looked after Muhammad ﷺ with a great deal of love and attention.
"You do not have to worry," she reassured the two of them, "Muhammad is a special child. I do not think the jinn can harm him."
Halima and Harith sighed with relief when they heard these words.
Even so, Amina did not have the heart to part with her son once again. "I want him to stay here," Amina said. "I am so happy that he is with me again."
And so Harith and Halima soon returned to the desert without their foster son.
It was not until several years later that they learned from Muhammad ﷺ what had actually happened on that special day in the desert: "The two figures in white garments were in fact not men but two angels," he explained. "They had brought a golden basin filled with glistening snow. They took my heart out of my chest and washed it with the snow. Then they put it back again and disappeared. It was not painful at all. Quite the contrary – it felt so wonderful."

Muhammad ﷺ and Amina greatly enjoyed the time they spent together in Mecca. Also, Muhammad soon made friends with his uncle Hamzah, who was his age.
When her son was six years old, Amina thought: "He is old enough now to travel to Yathrib with me and visit the grave of his father Abdullah." Besides, in Yathrib there lived some of her relatives who she wanted to see again. The city was several days' ride away from

Mecca. "We will join the next camel caravan leaving for Yathrib," Amina decided.
Soon Muhammad ﷺ and his mother, accompanied by their servant Baraka, were riding to Yathrib on two stately camels.
Having arrived there, Amina went to her husband's grave with her son. Lost in thought, she looked at the stony grave mound at her feet. She had spent only a few days with her beloved husband before he died quite unexpectedly. Muhammad ﷺ, standing at the grave side also greatly missed his father, whom he had never known.
For a whole month, Muhammad ﷺ and Amina stayed in Yathrib with their servant Baraka. Then Amina thought it was time to set off for home, but soon after they had started out, Amina suddenly felt ill. With each exhausting day travelling she lost more of her strength. Eventually she was unable to stay atop her camel's back any longer. Baraka was very worried about her mistress meanwhile. Near the village of Abwa the little group finally had to stop, since Amina's condition was getting worse and worse. Continuing the journey was out of the question. In the shade of a single palm tree, Baraka prepared a makeshift bed for Muhammad ﷺ and his mother. Baraka hoped that Amina would find some rest here. Exhausted, Amina sank down from the camel to the ground. When after a little while she opened her eyes and asked for water, she saw the worried faces of Muhammad ﷺ and Baraka. Amina felt the disease drain the last bit of strength from her. They would not see the end of this journey together. "My dear son," she whispered, "what was new will become old and what was

alive has to die some day, but I will be remembered forever because I gave birth to you."

Shortly afterwards Amina closed her eyes and passed away.

Full of compassion, Baraka tried to comfort the crying boy who had now become fully orphaned. After Amina had been buried, Baraka and little Muhammad ﷺ heavy-heartedly set out on their journey back to Mecca.

Abdul Muttalib

The Grandfather's Worries

From now on, Muhammad ﷺ lived with his grandfather Abdul Muttalib, who also grieved for Amina, his daughter-in-law. With great love and attention he now took care of his grandson. Almost every day the two of them could be seen together, walking hand in hand or sitting on a cushion in the shade of the Kaaba.

Abdul Muttalib was a member of the city's council of elders. He often took Muhammad along to the council meetings, where he asked him his opinion on the various topics that were being dealt with there. The other council members sneered at that, but Abdul Muttalib told them again and again, "That's no laughing matter. You will see: a great future lies ahead for my grandson."

At this time, Muhammad's grandfather was already more than eighty years old. Of course Abdul Muttalib knew that he was approaching the end of his life, and Muhammad ﷺ was far from being grown up, so he hoped that he would still be able to take care of his grandson for

as long as possible. But Amina had not even been dead for two years when one day the old man, lying on his bed, felt that his final hours had arrived. The time had come for him to bid farewell to the world. So he sent for his sons, Abu Lahab, Abu Talib, Hamza and Abbas, who soon afterwards gathered in their father's room. "I will not rise from this bed again," he told his sons. Abdul Muttalib had always faced the circumstances in his life with strength and fearlessness, but now bitter tears were running down his face. "I'm crying because soon I will no longer be able to embrace and protect Muhammad ﷺ," he added. "I'm so worried about my grandson. He doesn't have any one except me. I'm so afraid something might happen to this wonderful child."
"Do not worry about this," Abu Talib reassured him. "I will take

good care of him and watch over him," he promised. Abdul Muttalib looked his son right in the eyes. "I entrust him to your care," he declared, "and hand over the responsibility for him to you. If you want to make me happy, guard him and protect him like your own son, and treat him with love and respect as you always treated me."
Abu Talib promised to do everything to fulfil his father's last wish.
In this way Muhammad ﷺ got a new home once again. Abu Talib's wife Fatima loved children very much. She made every effort to be a good mother to her foster son. She wanted him to feel just as safe and secure in her home like her own children. So Muhammad ﷺ suddenly found himself in a big and cheerful family.
However it did not escape Muhammad's acute mind that his uncle had great difficulties feeding such a big family. Therefore he soon tried to provide for his own basic needs himself. He started herding goats in the mountains around Mecca for a small wage. In the searing heat of the day this was no easy task. But Muhammad ﷺ was not used to complaining. He responsibly looked after each one of the animals entrusted to him.
Abu Talib realised indeed how hard his nephew tried not to be a burden on his family. Muhammad ﷺ was a fast learner and was very conscientious in everything he did. "Perhaps he will become a good merchant," Abu Talib thought. He knew how much the boy wished he could travel with him every time Abu Talib planned to travel with a trade caravan. It had been the same this time, when he had mentioned his next business trip to Syria. "Please take me with you!"

Muhammad ﷺ had pleaded, but Abu Talib knew the dangers of a long ride through the desert, and he did not want to risk anything happening to his nephew. From sand storms and diseases up to assaults of armed robbers, all sorts of things could happen. “You are too young!” he had answered. “It’s better for you to stay with my brother Abbas until I come back.”

Soon a great caravan was passing through Mecca once again on its way to Syria. Lots of travellers had gathered in front of the Kaaba with their baggage and animals. The camel driver’s hoarse calls mixed with the sounds of the animals lowing and goats bleating. The scent of the animals‘ warm bodies was in the air. Camels were being loaded with crates and sacks.

Abu Talib had decided to join this caravan. The whole family had assembled around him to bid him farewell while he was mounting his camel. Suddenly Muhammad ﷺ was standing in front of him. “Please, Uncle, do take me with you!” he said quietly. When Abu Talib saw him like this, his heart was moved. How could he leave his boy behind just like that? Perhaps the time had come to let him gain some new experiences. After all, Muhammad ﷺ was no longer a little child. “Alright then,” Abu Talib agreed, “I’ll take you with me if you like!” His nephew had a great thirst for knowledge and he decided that he would teach him everything a good merchant needed to know.

A little while later, the uncle and his nephew were riding their camels, cleaving their way through the crowd at the Kaaba. A group of children were standing a little way away, curiously watching what was happening. A good many times, Muhammad ﷺ had stood there himself, watching the great caravans leaving the city. This time he would not stay behind. This time he would be part of them.

Bahira

Signs from Heaven

The caravan was approaching Bostra, a town in Syria which was home to a Christian monk. His name was Bahira, and he lived very modestly in a small and simple room. Probably nobody in Bostra would have guessed that he of all people had a special treasure hidden in his room. It was a crate full of ancient and very valuable scriptures that had secretly been handed down from monk to monk for many years. So many times had he read these writings that he almost knew them by heart. They told of things that were to happen one day, perhaps very soon. One of the scriptures announced the appearance of a prophet among the Arabs. A new prophet – sent by God! A messenger, endowed with divine knowledge, who came to teach people and set an example for them. Someone who would bring answers to all the vital questions. "My God," the monk pleaded, "I ask you to fulfil your humblest servant's only wish: permit me to witness the arrival of your messenger!"

His whole life Bahira had been praying in this way, and many years had passed since then. Every day he looked out for the signs that were announced in the old scriptures. And so on that day he was watching the hustle and bustle around him as on all the other days. People did not take much notice of him. They had no idea what was going on in the mind of the old monk, and most of them were probably not interested. This would certainly have been different if they had known what Bahira saw from the place where he was sitting. On that day, the monk discovered something very exceptional indeed: one single little cloud was floating in the bright blue sky. This might have happened sometimes, even if it was a little unusual, but this cloud was not blown by the wind but seemed to be following a caravan so that the travellers could walk in its shade. Bahira's heart almost missed a beat. "The time has come!" he thought. "This must be a sign. At last!" He jumped to his feet excitedly and hurried towards the caravan that was approaching. "Welcome to Bostra!" he greeted the travellers. "You must be tired and hungry from the long journey. Therefore I would like to invite you to have dinner with me. Please be my guests tonight and do not leave anyone behind!"

How hungry the men were! Nobody wanted to miss the invitation. And so it did not take long until they had gathered at the friendly monk's home. Bahira eyed each of them intently. But none of them suited the description he had found in his old books. "Something must be wrong," Bahira thought. "Did anyone stay behind perhaps?" "Men of Quraysh," he said, "I want each one of you to eat. None of

you is to stay behind and be hungry." "We really haven't left anyone behind," one of the men replied, "except for a boy to look after the animals." This boy was Muhammad ﷺ, the youngest member of the caravan. Abu Talib had by now regretted not to have brought his nephew to dinner. "I'll send for him," he said, "it won't be long."

Shortly afterwards Muhammad ﷺ entered the room. At the first glance Bahira sensed that he had now found the right person. While they were eating, he began to ask the boy questions as unobtrusively as possible. "What is your name?" the old monk asked. "Where are you from and which tribe do you belong to?" Muhammad ﷺ replied politely, as was his way. "My name is Muhammad," he said, "I am from Mecca and I belong to the tribe of Quraysh."

Bahira's excitement grew stronger. This was the reply he had hoped for. So he asked some more questions that were all answered to his satisfaction. To be really sure, however, it was imperative for Bahira to see the boy's back.

Muhammad ﷺ did not mind when Bahira asked him if he could take a look. The monk saw the oval mark right away. Now he was completely certain: this boy had been chosen by God. One day his prophethood would become apparent! The old monk was overjoyed. At the same time he was afraid of what would happen if people were to find out what was special about Muhammad ﷺ. To spread the word of God was a difficult task. Most of the earlier prophets had been relentlessly persecuted by their opponents. Now Muhammad ﷺ was still a little boy, but one day he would no longer be overlooked!

Bahira waited for the right moment to take Abu Talib aside. "Take him back to your country and protect him!" Bahira whispered urgently. "By God, if people come to know what I know about him they will try to harm him as much as possible. Your nephew is someone special. Just wait and see – a lot of extraordinary things will happen around him. You are responsible for him. I am telling you: you have to protect him!"

The Kaaba

The Dispute about the Black Stone

The long period of drought was over. At last the gates of the sky opened up again and the first fat raindrops reached the earth. Fresh and cool they splashed onto the parched plain of Mecca. All the people were relieved. Rain at last! After a few minutes the heavenly blessing was drumming onto the roofs of the whole city. The surrounding mountains began to dissolve in the grey colour of the rain.

The parched soil, however, had become so hard from sun and heat that it could not take up this amount of water at all. Instead, the rain water was flowing from the mountains in brownish trickles down towards the valley. The thin trickles quickly grew into brooks, and eventually the water was rushing down from the mountains in streams. The mighty floods damaged the houses of Mecca and even caused whole buildings to collapse. But the inhabitants of Mecca were tough people; they were used to cope with difficult situations. Life in this region had always been like that. Sometimes the forces of

nature seemed to run riot in the desert; sweltering heat and extreme droughts alternated with floodings and sandstorms.
When things had started to quieten down, the Meccans set out to examine the damage. Terrified, they noticed that this time even the Kaaba had been severely damaged. At first no one dared to set their hands to the holy house, but soon it became apparent that they had no other choice. Apart from the foundations, all the walls of the Kaaba had to be rebuilt, so they started to remove the stones one by one. As there were lots of helping hands, the construction work at the Kaaba was proceeding briskly. Soon the men had worked their way to the large Black Stone that was embedded in the wall on one of the corners of the building.
It was a very special stone, for it was ancient and originated from Paradise. When it had come to Earth, it had been completely white and pure – whiter still than snow. Whoever touched or even kissed the stone felt relief. Allah had sent it down to Earth for people to remember Paradise. But over the centuries, people's many bad thoughts and deeds darkened the stone until it finally turned deep black.
Now the men had to temporarily remove even this special stone from the wall. Later on it was to be put back in its old place. Up to this point the men had worked together well, but then they suddenly began to quarrel over whose right it was to put the Black Stone back in its place. The argument smoldered for several days and no agreement was in sight. Each tribe wanted to prevail; none of those involved

wanted to cave in. Soon the whole issue started to get out of control. The men got more and more hotheaded. They began to yell at each other and insult each other. Eventually the tribesmen of Abd ad-Dar even brought a bowl of animal blood and dipped their hands into it

with the intention of threatening the others. Abu Umayyah was the eldest of those present. When he saw the men goading each other, he feared that the whole matter was indeed going to end in violence and bloodshed. If he could only come up with something! Finally he called "Stop it! Men of Quraysh, I want to make a suggestion: let your dispute be decided by the next man to come in through the gate." In surprise, the men paused in their quarrel. At last somebody had a good idea! The men agreed, and they were curious to see who would be the one to come through the gate next.

The men did not have to wait long at all: the first one to enter the gate was Muhammad ﷺ. "Thank God!" Abu Umayyah sighed. If the men were going to listen to somebody at all, it would be him. He heard them calling "It is al-Amin, the Trustworthy!" They explained the point at issue to Muhammad ﷺ. He deliberated for a moment; between the two parties there was a notable tension in the air. Which of the tribes would he decide for?

"Bring me a sturdy cloth," Muhammad suddenly requested. "What's that good for?" the men grumbled. But after all they had agreed to listen to their advisor. So someone went to fetch a cloth. They spread the fabric on the ground. Muhammad ﷺ gently placed the Black Stone in its centre. Then he said, "Each one of you takes hold of the cloth on one side. In this way, you can put the stone in the right spot in the wall all together."

The men looked at each other in surprise. What a brilliant idea! Avidly, they set to work. Muhammad ﷺ himself pushed the stone in place in the end. The men cheered, and Abu Umayyah beamed with relief. "How easily this could have gone wrong!" he thought. "How lucky we are to have Muhammad ﷺ in our midst!"

Khadidja

A Happy Wedding

Khadijah lived in one of the greatest and most beautiful houses in Mecca. From here she conducted her trading business. She organised caravans and arranged for goods to be sold or exchanged.

Khadijah was one of the richest women in the city. She was also beautiful and intelligent. Aside from that, she was independent and able to decide freely on many matters. Khadijah knew that she was very fortunate in this respect. She usually was even able to gain respect from men, and there was no lack of marriage proposals.

Most of the women in Mecca admired her. More than a few would have traded lives with Khadijah without the slightest hesitation.

But Khadijah had suffered several blows of fate, too. She was already forty years of age and had been married twice. Sadly, both marriages had been childless.

She had been a widow for quite some time now, and organising the business alone was not an easy feat. Every day new decisions had to

be taken, and she constantly had to stand up to men, for they were not at all used to following the orders of a woman. Moreover, she had to bear responsibility for many people; the families of Khadijah's servants and employees were dependent on the wages she paid them. If problems arose among the people who worked for her, she was the one who had to try and find a solution. Thus, she occasionally considered a marriage proposal, but she found it difficult to picture any of the many men who asked for her hand as a husband, so she continued to arrange her affairs on her own.

One day Khadijah was urgently looking for someone reliable to lead a great caravan. She was advised to hire young Muhammad ﷺ, who was renowned for his honesty and was therefore called "al-Amin", the Trustworthy, by everyone. Khadijah had already heard people speak of Muhammad ﷺ several times by then.
"He is certainly the right one for my task!" Khadijah deliberated. She decided to engage the promising young man as leader for her caravan.
She was willing to pay him double the normal wage and in addition to place one of her own servants at his disposal for the journey.
But beforehand, Khadijah wanted to make sure that she had actually chosen the right person. After all, as the caravan leader Muhammad ﷺ would bear responsibility for a great number of people and animals, not to mention the precious goods he would be carrying.
So she sent off one of her messengers in order to make an offer to Muhammad ﷺ and to talk the matter over with him. As Khadijah was mindful of her good reputation, she invited Muhammad's aunt Atika to come too. Shortly afterwards the two visitors were at the door. "Please come in," Khadijah greeted them. "Welcome to my house!"
In all her life, Khadijah had never met such an exceptional young man.
The most striking thing about him was this radiance. There was a unique light on his face. Muhammad ﷺ had brown eyes, framed by long lashes. There was a depth and a power in his gaze that Khadijah

had never before noticed in any other person. When he smiled at her, it seemed to her as if he could look deeply into her soul.

After this encounter, Khadijah was absolutely sure of one thing: she had found the person she had always longed for. But would he feel the same way?

Muhammad ﷺ accepted Khadijah's offer of work and was therefore entrusted with the leadership of the great trade caravan.

Khadijah was very curious how the journey would pass. And so a couple of weeks later she was impatiently waiting for the return of the caravan. She had already gone up on the roof of her house several times to see if the silhouettes of the camels with their riders would finally appear at the horizon.

A letter which her servant Maysara had sent in advance had already informed her about some issues. Young Muhammad ﷺ had turned out to be a great leader and merchant who did excellent business. She would be able to resell the goods he brought for double the buying price in Mecca. At last a messenger announced the approach of the caravan. Soon afterwards the servant and a little later Muhammad ﷺ entered the house to report the outcome of the trade journey.

In spite of all the good news, Khadijah was hardly able to follow the conversation – her heart was beating so excitedly.

"I wonder if he would marry me," Khadijah said to herself. She felt that her wealth would certainly not impress him. Perhaps her beauty or her character would. However, she was fifteen years his senior. For sure Muhammad ﷺ had younger women to choose from.

Khadijah told her friend Nufaysa what had happened. Nufaysa was full of confidence. She already had an idea how to subtly act as a mediator without putting her friend in an embarrassing situation. She went up to Muhammad ﷺ and asked him, "Why don't you get married?" "Because I do not earn enough to sustain a family," he replied. "And what if I suggest marrying a person who herself would contribute enough wealth, possession and beauty to your marriage – would you be willing to consider again?" Nufaysa went on.

"Who would this marriage be with?" Muhammad ﷺ asked in surprise.

"With the noble woman Khadijah," she replied.

"I would be exceptionally happy about this," Muhammad ﷺ answered, "but why should she agree to such an unfavourable relationship? Certainly there must be quite a few other suitors who can offer her many things for which I do not have the means."

"Leave it to me," Nufaysa said shrewdly. With her good news, Nufaysa immediately returned to Khadijah, who meanwhile had questioned her servant Maysara once again to learn more about his journey with Muhammad ﷺ. Maysara had narrated astonishing stories to her: Bahira, the monk from Bostra, had died. His place had been taken by another monk since, who had approached Maysara. "He told me to listen carefully to what Muhammad ﷺ says, for he would be the future Prophet of God!" Maysara recounted. "But that's not all. All through the journey I had been wondering why the sun did not bother us at all. Somehow it was always pleasantly cool. Then one day at noon I suddenly realised why this was so. Imagine – for a brief moment I could see two huge angels above our heads. They were protecting Muhammad ﷺ from the sun with their wings!" Khadijah knew that Maysara was telling the truth, for she trusted him entirely. Besides, when she had watched the caravan's arrival from the roof of her house, she herself had thought for a moment that she had discerned a wing-like shape above the heads of the camel riders. There were so many peculiar signs in connection with Muhammad ﷺ. In any case, he seemed to be under a special, divine protection.

Khadijah was aware that Muhammad ﷺ could not ask for her hand of his own accord, because he did not have the means to do so. It would look as if he would want to marry her in order to acquire her riches. So she herself had to take the first step. Khadijah was a courageous woman. Therefore she soon asked Muhammad ﷺ to visit her and told him, "I have loved you since the day we first met; not only because you are my relative, but above all because you have such a beautiful character. I love you because you always take a stand for justice and want the best for all people, and because you are so honest."

The sincerity and love in Khadijah's words moved Muhammad ﷺ a great deal. With delight and happiness, he accepted her hand. He confidently promised to discuss the matter with his uncle Abu Talib. When Abu Talib heard the good news, he was very glad about the unexpected turn of events in his nephew's life and at once gave him his blessing.

In order for the events to take the right course, Khadijah's cousin Waraqah had to be asked for his consent, too. Compared to Khadijah,

Muhammad ﷺ only had a small income. Thus it was actually possible that Waraqah would not consider him a suitable match for his rich cousin. Therefore the marriage negotiations had to be carried out as cleverly as possible. Muhammad's uncle Hamzah seemed to be particularly suitable for this task, as his sister Safiyya was married to Khadijah's brother.

So shortly afterwards Hamzah set out for the house of Abu Talib, who was hosting guests that evening and had invited him and Waraqah to join them. Later that evening, after the men had been sitting together for a while, Hamzah cautiously began to talk about his request.

"Dear Waraqah," he began, "you know what a wonderful person Muhammad is. He is absolutely trustworthy, amiable and honest…"

When Hamzah saw the benevolent expression on the face of the man opposite him, he decided to complete the request he was about to make: "On behalf of Muhammad, I ask you for Khadijah's hand."

"You have my consent," the old man said, beaming. "Believe me - nothing would make me happier than the two of them getting married! But first I'll have to ask Khadijah if she agrees as well." Hamzah and Waraqah agreed upon a dowry of 20 she-camels to Khadijah.

And soon Muhammad ﷺ and Khadijah happily celebrated their wedding.

Waraqah

A Blind Man Receives a Visitor

Waraqah was straining his ears to listen into the darkness. Had somebody knocked on the door? Indeed, there was a noise at the door. He did not really expect any visitors. A few moments later, however, his cousin Khadijah was there, greeting him: "All hail, Waraqah!"

In an instant, Waraqah noticed the unusual quivering in her voice – like the sound of a fluttering bird. Khadijah was fifty-five years old now, but Waraqah had never before perceived even the slightest insecurity in her voice, although he was a master of these things. The eternal darkness that surrounded him had taught Waraqah to clearly distinguish the sounds and odours of the world. Therefore he used to experience many things that escaped those who could see. But in this case his blindness did not make any difference; even a seeing person would instantly have noticed Khadijah's agitation.

She was trembling. Waraqah sensed that something must have happened to Muhammad ﷺ.

Khadijah and Muhammad ﷺ were very happy together, they had a big family to provide for. In the course of the years, Khadijah had given birth to two sons and four daughters. Sadly, the two boys had died very young.

Also, one of Abu Talib's sons lived with Khadijah and Muhammad ﷺ. And then there was Zayd, the slave boy, whom Muhammad ﷺ had first set free and then, upon the boy's own request, had adopted him as a son.

Moreover, Muhammad ﷺ and Khadijah of course continued to support Halima, his foster mother, as much as they could. Luckily, Muhammad ﷺ did good business so that he had sufficient means. Generosity was one of his outstanding qualities. That month, Muhammad ﷺ had already been fasting for many days, and he distributed the meals he had not eaten during his fast to poor people. Neighbours and friends often came by and asked him for advice, and Muhammad ﷺ always had a prudent and wise answer. Most of the Meccans appreciated his advice very much. And yet, in the past few months, Waraqah had clearly felt that Muhammad ﷺ had changed.

His cousin's husband had become forty years of age this year. Lately, he had often climbed up alone to a secluded rock cave high up at Jabal Noor, the mountain of light. He would sit there for hours, thinking and praying. Waraqah also knew that Muhammad ﷺ had unusual dreams – dreams that came true. For some time there had even been rumours going around that were related to him; they said that Muhammad ﷺ could be the new Prophet, a deliverer of divine messages.

"If there is any man at all who deserves this honour it certainly is Muhammad," Waraqah thought.
From the beginning, Khadijah had been Muhammad's closest confidante. To her he could entrust the things he had witnessed. Now Khadijah herself seemed to be in need of advice. Whatever had happened? Waraqah asked his cousin Khadijah to take a seat. And then he listened attentively to what she told him.

The Night of Power

The Revelation of the Angel

"Muhammad climbed up the mountain again last night," Khadijah reported. "Up there in the rocks there is a cave called Hira, where it is always cool and quiet. There in the darkness of the cave one does not hear anything but the beating of one's own heart. Muhammad sat down on the stony ground and began to pray.

Hour after hour he spent in this way while outside the stars were shining in the sky. He finally got very tired and fell asleep. It was well into the night when something odd happened: Muhammad woke up from his sleep and opened his eyes, blinking a few times. The next moment he rose with a start - the entire cave was bathed in blazing light, and a mighty figure was coming towards Muhammad.

'This must be an angel,' Muhammad thought. The angel was holding a piece of the finest cloth in his hand. He held it in front of his face and said, 'Read!' But Muhammad did not know how to read. So he said, 'I cannot read!' The angel, however, could not be dissuaded. He grabbed Muhammad's arm and commanded again, 'Read!' – 'But I cannot read,' Muhammad replied again. Then the angel grabbed him even more fiercely, almost strangling him with the cloth, and commanded again, 'Read!'

Finally, Muhammad called out in despair: 'What shall I read?'

So the angel began to speak:

﴾ *In the name of Allah, the Beneficent, the Merciful*
Read! In the name of your Lord Who created –
Created man out of a clot.
Read! And your Lord is Most Generous,
He Who taught by the pen,-
Taught man that which he knew not. ﴿
(Surah 96, Verses 1-5)

Muhammad repeated all the verses word by word and tried to memorise everything well. After he had done so, the angel disappeared. Light-headed, Muhammad left the cave and hurried down the mountain towards the valley. You can imagine how agitated he was.

As he was on his way, he was assailed by doubts and thought, 'Maybe this was no angel after all but an evil spirit that wants to drive me mad!'

Before he reached the valley, Muhammad heard a resounding voice. 'Muhammad, you are the one whom God will send to the people with his message,' the voice said. 'You are the messenger of God, and I am Jibril!'

Muhammad stopped in order to see where the voice came from. Then he saw the angel in his true size, standing at the horizon with his wings spread.

The angel filled the whole sky. No matter which way Muhammad turned – he saw him everywhere: in the North, the South, the East, and the West.

From this moment on, Muhammad was certain: this huge being full of light was indeed the Angel Jibril."

Khadijah took a deep breath, and then she continued her story. "I'm telling you, when Muhammad arrived at home, his heart was pounding so loud that I thought it would burst!" she went on. "Muhammad beseeched me again and again: 'Cover me! Cover me!' After I had covered him, it still took quite a while until he calmed down. Then he told me the whole story. At the end, he said to me, 'Khadijah, I'm in fear of my life!' I wanted to reassure him, so I answered, 'Allah will certainly not abandon you. You are always so helpful and hospitable, and you come to the aid of everyone who is in need.'"

Khadijah fell silent, pondering. Then she turned to her cousin again: "Waraqah, please do tell me: what do you think of the whole matter?"

Waraqah had remained silent throughout the narrative. Before his mind's eye, he still saw the images of Muhammad ﷺ and the angel. While he was thinking about the angel's words, it suddenly struck him like lightning. "Holy! Holy!", he exclaimed. "By Him in whose hands is my soul! If what you have said is true, then Muhammad has indeed met the Angel Jibril up there in the cave! It is the same angel who came to the Prophet Moses a long time ago. Oh Khadijah, Allah has chosen your husband for a special task. He is a prophet, a messenger of God! With Allah's help he will lead people to the right path."

For a moment, Waraqah was torn between a feeling of concern for Muhammad ﷺ and the joy over what had happened. Waraqah knew the stories of all the previous prophets' lives by heart. None of them had had it easy. Despite this all, Waraqah felt joy. Muhammad ﷺ was a prophet! What difference did it make that he himself was blind and old, if he could live at the side of God's Prophet?
Shortly afterwards Waraqah met Muhammad ﷺ at the Kaaba, where he asked him to relate what had happened that night on the mountain.
When Muhammad ﷺ had ended his narrative, Waraqah reaffirmed his conviction, which he had expressed before to Khadijah: "By Him in whose hands is my soul. The Angel Jibril visited you, just as he came to Moses long ago. You are the new Prophet!" Then he added, "But you have to be on your guard! People will certainly claim that you are lying. They will certainly try to insult and banish you, maybe even to kill you." "You really think this could happen?" Muhammad whispered with concern. "I am afraid so," Waraqah sighed, "for no messenger has ever been able to fulfil his task without being rejected and persecuted for it. But I promise you: if I live to see that day, I will be on your side."

The Prayer

Longing for Allah

Muhammad's first encounter with the Angel Jibril took place one night in the month of Ramadan. Soon afterwards, a verse was revealed which dealt with that night:

﴾ In the name of Allah, the Beneficent, the Merciful.
We have indeed revealed this (Message) in the Night of Power.
And what will explain to thee what the Night or Power is?
The Night of Power is better than a thousand months.
Therein come down the angels and the Spirit
by Allah's permission, on every errand:
Peace it is until the emergence of dawn. ﴿
(Surah 97, Verses 1-5)

Khadijah did not have the slightest doubt that the words Muhammad ﷺ had heard really originated from God. "I believe you!" his beloved wife assured him repeatedly. "Let me be the first one to be taught that which was revealed to you."

One day, Jibril appeared on a hill near Mecca while Muhammad ﷺ was there. The Angel stamped his foot to make a hole. At once, fresh water gushed out of it. With this water, the Angel showed Muhammad ﷺ how to make ablution before praying. Muhammad ﷺ watched the Angel closely, then he made ablution just the way the Angel had shown him. After that, the Angel positioned himself for prayer. Muhammad ﷺ stood next to him. During the prayer they touched the ground with their foreheads several times, praying silently to themselves, and whenever Muhammad ﷺ called on God, his words came from the bottom of his heart:

"Oh Allah, I ask you for good fortune and blessing! Protect me from all adversities and from ruin. I ask you to help me remember your words and recite them correctly. Oh Allah, please always let me be grateful and always let my feet walk on the right path. Oh Allah, please protect me from the hellfire and surround me with the scents of heaven instead."

Back home the Prophet showed this new way of praying to his wife Khadijah first. As time went on, Muhammad ﷺ also began to speak in public about the knowledge which Jibril conveyed to him. "Believe in God!" he told the people he encountered, and he recited to them what Allah had revealed to him:

﴾ *He is the One who rendered the sun radiant,*
And the moon a light,
And He designed its phases
That you may learn to count the years and to calculate.
Allah did not create all this, except for a specific purpose.
He explains the revelations for people who know.
Surely, in the alternation of night and day,
And what Allah created
In the heavens and the earth,
There are proofs for people who are righteous. ﴿
(Surah 10, Verses 5/6)

Many people were deeply touched by the Prophet's words. When Muhammad ﷺ was reciting, they suddenly felt some of the splendour and the grandness of the divine. Their longing grew so great that it made them weep. It sometimes even happened that people were so awestruck by the sound of the heavenly verses that they fell in a faint. "How does Muhammad know such unique verses?" people were wondering. "He doesn't even know how to read and write!?"

Soon more and more people were following the teachings of the new Prophet. They removed the old idols from their home altars and threw them into the fire. From then on, they wanted to pray to the one and unseen God only, the God whom Muhammad ﷺ told them about and whom they called Allah.

Uthman

The Mysterious Voice

A lonely camel rider was resting on a blanket in the shade of a tree. His name was Uthman and he was a merchant on his way from Syria to Mecca. He was exhausted from the heat of the day and glad the few twigs above his head gave him some shade.

Sleep had just begun to cool down his eye lids when suddenly he thought he heard a voice call him. "Sleeper, wake up!" the voice called. "Ahmad has appeared in Mecca." Surprised, the merchant opened his eyes and leapt to his feet. What was that strange voice he had just heard? Uthman glanced around in confusion, looking in every direction. All the sounds and traces in the desert were familiar to him. But nothing seemed to indicate that a human being had been near.

"Was this just a dream?" he wondered. "And if it was a dream, what is it supposed to mean? Ahmad, the Highly Praised One…," Uthman deliberated, "who might that be?" There was no thought of sleep

now. Lost in thoughts, he folded his blanket and grabbed his camel's reins.
So the lonely rider started out on his way again, the shimmering horizon in front of him. Silvery mirages were gleaming on the sandy plain like a shiny water surface. Again and again, Uthman thought about his dream. But he was not able to figure out its meaning.
A while later, Uthman met an acquaintance named Talha, and the two men greeted each other joyously. After they had been talking for a while, Talha related his encounter with a monk in the town of Bostra. "The monk asked me a peculiar question: he wanted to know if Ahmad had already revealed himself as a prophet. 'Who is Ahmad?' I asked him. The old man said to me: 'Ahmad, the Highly Praised One, is Abdul Muttalib's grandson. God has chosen him to make him His messenger.'"
In surprise, Uthman remembered the voice in the desert. Was he to learn in this way what it was all about? Excitedly he told Uthman in his turn what he had heard while resting under the tree. "Abdul Muttalib's grandson named Ahmad…? This can only be Muhammad!" he exclaimed. Now he was perfectly sure: the voice that had called him was a divine sign.
Together the two men set off to meet Muhammad ﷺ. When a short time later Uthman stood in front of Muhammad ﷺ, he did not hesitate – having received all those signs - to acknowledge Muhammad ﷺ as God's Prophet.

"I bear witness that there is no God but Allah and that you, Muhammad, are his Prophet!" he said. Talha did the same, for he did not have any doubt either. However, not all people in Mecca wanted to believe in the heavenly origin of Muhammad's messages.

Abu Talib

Unbidden Guests

Abu Talib mindfully observed the change that had been going on within his nephew. He could not really believe in this unseen God that Muhammad ﷺ was constantly talking about. Most people in Mecca did not believe in God. Therefore they were not afraid of Him and much less so of hell. Abu Talib had to admit: the law of the strongest was all that counted in Mecca. Whoever was rich and strong got away with everything, and the poor and weak ones were glad if they survived at all. Abu Talib could not recall a time when this had been different. Muhammad ﷺ - that much he was sure of – had always detested this way of life. Meanwhile his nephew pointed out these wrongs in public; apparently this unseen God had requested him to do so. "I am here to bear good tidings," Muhammad ﷺ stated, "but I have also come to warn you! One day God will hold each one of you accountable for their deeds."

Every day Muhammad ﷺ encouraged people to show more compassion towards those in need of help. "First and foremost, take care of the orphans!" he reminded them over and over. Many of them had no home and survived by begging in the streets. But there were also other people in Mecca who were in great need, among them a number of women whose husbands had divorced them or died. Very often they had no possibility of feeding themselves and providing for themselves sufficiently. Never did Muhammad ﷺ go to sleep at night before he had given out even the last dinar he had. He had always been extremely generous, and his marriage to Khadijah had not changed this. Above all, however, he declared himself to be against

the custom of slaying newborn girls. To have a son was regarded a great honour in Mecca; a boy was able to contribute in providing for the family at an early age. To raise a girl, however, was considered a burden, even a shame. Thus, many girls were killed right after they were born. Muhammad ﷺ was deeply horrified every time he heard of such a case. His wife Khadijah supported him in his endeavours to prevent these abominable deeds. But it soon became apparent that this was no easy task.

Abu Talib soon watched the people of Mecca split into two camps. Some were enthusiastic about Muhammad's teachings. They felt how great his love of God and the people was and recognised a deep truth in everything he tried to convey to them. They admired him for standing up for his views so bravely, although in doing so he had to defy the most powerful men in Mecca. Among those who followed him were lots of young people, for their minds and hearts were still open. Abu Talib had a lot of understanding for them. The other Meccans, however, began to feel more and more annoyed by his nephew. Up to a short while ago, they all had liked him a great deal, but the things he had recently said clearly went too far in their opinion. So some people became extremely hostile towards Muhammad ﷺ. They insulted him in the foulest way and even declared him to be mad. Yet, Khadijah stood by him, she comforted and encouraged Muhammad ﷺ; without consolation from her he certainly would have been close to despair at times.

With all these things going on, Abu Talib was not at all surprised when one day several men came and knocked on his door. They were led by Abu Jahl, Muhammad's fiercest opponent. One of the men said to Abu Talib, "Your nephew is inciting our own children to turn on us! Everything we hear now is 'Muhammad said this, Muhammad said that.' Where is this leading to?" Another man said, "If everyone believes in that one unseen God, what will happen to our god statues in the Kaaba? Mecca lives, as we know, on the revenues we gain from the pilgrims who come here every year to visit our idols. What will happen to the offering money? People are not likely to pay for a God they don't see". Another one said, "We are afraid that Muhammad is going to turn the slaves on us. Soon they will refuse to do their work. Yesterday, he even told us to treat the slaves like our brothers. I have never heard anything as crazy as this!"

At first, the men were behaving rather politely, but when they realised that their words did not have the desired effect on Abu Talib, they expressed themselves more clearly: "Tell him that we are not going to tolerate him mocking our customs and speaking ill of our gods! Make him stop all this if you do not want anything to happen to you and your nephew!"

They actually dared to threaten him! Abu Talib knew the men well enough to know that he had better take their threat seriously. With concern, he went to see his nephew. He definitely had to tell him about the incident.

Muhammad ﷺ listened to his account. Quitting was out of the question for him. After considering the issue for a moment he stood up and said, ",O my uncle, by Allah, if they put the sun in my right hand and the moon in my left in return for my giving up this cause, I would not give it up until Allah makes Truth victorious, or I die in His service". Abu Talib could not help admitting to himself that he was proud of his nephew's courage, even if he did not actually share his views. But he was also aware of the fact that this answer would have serious consequences.

Muhammad ﷺ detested any form of violence, but his opponents would not shy away from resorting to the most terrible means of silencing him.

With a sense of foreboding, Abu Talib soon set out to go back home.

Bilal

A Slave Plucks up Courage

Bilal had been living in his master Umayyah's household for a long time. He had got used to his work and knew exactly what he had to do. Whenever he was called to his master, he carried out every task silently and diligently. Bilal had been born a slave. He did not even own his black skin; however he was glad he did not have to suffer hunger – in this regard he could have been worse off. Unfortunately though, his mistress took delight in mortifying or harassing him out of the blue. Bilal never knew what kind of injustice would hit him next. His master Umayyah did not show quite the same unpredictability as his wife. But once he got annoyed at something, he could become particularly brutal. Most of the slaves in his house had already got acquainted with their master Umayyah's leather whip. This behaviour was the reason why Bilal did his best to maintain a low profile; one might even say Bilal tried to make himself invisible – a difficult task, considering his extraordinary height.

One day, guests had been invited to Umayyah's house. Plenty of wine was served, and there was a lot of talk. Soon the conversations turned into an excited discussion. As was often the case now, it was all about the new religion that was propagated in Mecca by a man named Muhammad. Its followers called themselves Muslims. Their religion was called "Islam", meaning "submission to God". "Peace" is also part of the meaning of this word. Bilal had frequently heard Muhammad's name in different discussions recently. Every time this name was mentioned, his master Umayyah got upset.

Suddenly the front door was pushed open. Bilal watched a young man harshly being shoved into the room. When Umayyah became aware of him, his face darkened. The master of the house did not even try to suppress his anger. He planted himself in front of the young man threateningly and took him to task. Bilal realised that this young man must be a follower of Muhammad's religion.

Infuriated, Umayyah exclaimed, "So Muhammad claims that every human being is worth the same, whether man or woman, slave or free man? I bought that black slave over there for a sackful of dinars on the market. I own him. And you, Ammar, son of Yassir, mean to say he is worth the same as me, his master?"

"Yes, I do!" the young man answered patiently but firmly. "Muhammad says that all people are equal before God, like the teeth of a comb."

While Ammar was speaking, he looked at Bilal in a friendly way.

Umayyah's face was distorted with rage, the room was deadly silent. "You show him!" Umayyah hissed. "You show him, Bilal! Show him the difference between a master and his slave. I want him to know and feel who is the master here." With these words, he thrust the leather whip into Bilal's hand. "Flog him! Quick, get started!" he urged. Ammar comprehended at once how dangerous the situation was for the slave. "Do what he says," he whispered, "or he is going to kill you! You have to do it!"

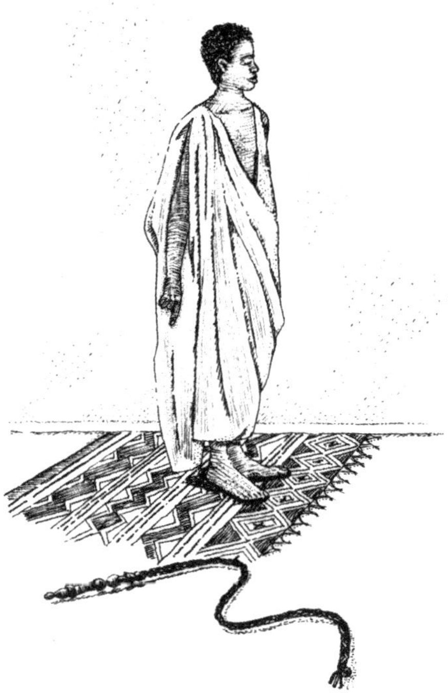

But Bilal did not move. This young man had mustered up the courage to tell the truth to the faces of the powerful men of the city. And now he was even going to put up with whippings so as not to jeopardise him, a black slave. "Do what he says!" Ammar implored him once again. "Come on!"

But Bilal did not move. Tears were burning in his eyes. "All people are equal before God, like the teeth of a comb." Like water in the desert sand, these words were seeping into the slave's heart; there they turned into a torrent. It was as if the entire sorrow of his life, accumulated over the years, were to break out of him at once. Bilal suddenly knew that his life had reached a turning point. For the first time in a long while he straightened up to his full height. He felt as strong as never before. And the best thing about it was that he was no longer afraid!

The leather whip fell down in front of Umayyah's feet with a rumbling noise. Bilal was not going to flog this young man. And he was never going to hide again either!

Hamza

A Fight for the Prophet

Hamzah urged his horse on. He briskly galloped across the plains heading towards Mecca. Lately he felt uneasy whenever he had to leave the city for extended periods of time. Since Muhammad ﷺ had begun to circulate those unusual verses, he constantly got into difficulties. Muhammad ﷺ insisted that it was the Angel Jibril himself who taught him these words. Admittedly, he himself had also had doubts at the beginning, but Muhammad ﷺ had never told a single lie in his whole life. Besides, that he should have thought up such lines was inconceivable.

One could indeed witness inexplicable things near his nephew Muhammad ﷺ: once, for example, he had stroked the leg of a lame goat, and immediately it could walk again. It was obvious that Muhammad ﷺ was not like all the others. Most Meccans had also noticed this over the years. Yet, by no means were all of them ready to believe that an angel appeared to him and dictated words to him.

The contents of those words, after all, were turning the entire old order upside down. Not everyone wanted to accept that the old gods should suddenly be replaced by one single God, or that a woman or a slave should be equivalent to a free man.

The thought of this reminded Hamzah of the matter of Bilal, the black slave. As expected, Bilal had been punished severely for his disobedience. His master Umayyah had had him tie to the stony ground and rolled a huge rock on his chest. Then he had left him there in the midday heat! In spite of his pain, Bilal had exclaimed again and again, "There is only one God! There is only one God!"

Abu Bakr decided to make an end to this atrocity. So he turned to Umayyah, "Are you not afraid that Allah will punish you for what you are doing to poor Bilal? How far do you want to go?" "You only have yourself to blame," Umayyah replied impassively. "After all, you were the one who spoiled him." Abu Bakr offered two hundred dinars to pitiless Umayyah in exchange for the slave.

Finally Umayyah had agreed. Two hundred dinars were a lot of money for a rebellious slave after all.

Abu Bakr set Bilal free at once, as was typical for him. He had bought other slaves before only to set them free afterwards.

Umayyah would certainly not forget the humiliation he suffered when Bilal defied him until the end. Hamzah was wondering what the next aggravation would be that Umayyah and his supporters would contrive to carry out against the believers. The situation in Mecca became more and more precarious.

Muhammad ﷺ went to the Kaaba several times every day. While circling it, he was constantly saying his prayers quietly. In doing so, he meanwhile received angry looks and even abuses from others more and more often. One time someone had even sneaked up to the Prophet from behind and pushed his turban from his head, so that it fell down in the sand in front of Muhammad ﷺ. Hamzah's face darkened when he remembered this. Muhammad ﷺ was simply too good-natured. Why on earth did he put up with all that?
A short while later the lonely rider reached the city. When he turned his gaze towards the Kaaba, he instantly realised the crowd of people in front of it. Hamzah spurred his horse on even more – hopefully nothing bad had happened! Suddenly a woman called out something to him. Hamzah reined the horse in and came to a stop next to her. In agitation, she told him what she had just witnessed:

"When I came, Muhammad ﷺ was sitting next to the Kaaba. Since he was deeply immersed in his prayer, he apparently did not notice Abu Jahl approaching him and positioning himself on the hill of Safa next to the Kaaba. Suddenly Abu Jahl took a stone in his hand and aimed it at Muhammad ﷺ. I really have never seen something as treacherous as this!" the woman ranted. "He hurt Muhammad on his head! As usual, Muhammad ﷺ did not breathe a word. He simply went home in silence."

Hamzah was usually a very friendly man, but he was also strong like a lion. When it came to winning a fight, he could be quite resolute. And he had a strong dislike for injustices. Right now he was burning with anger. "From today on I also confess to Muhammad's religion," he yelled, as he approached Abu Jahl threateningly. "If you want to keep on offending him, brawl with me!" With these words he dealt him a heavy blow. Abu Jahl was normally no coward, but in this case he knew he had better run away. This was a fight he could not win!

The Boycott

The Miracle of the Boycott Document

It was a heavy blow for Muhammad's adversaries that Hamzah, the Lion, had sided with Muhammad ﷺ. They no longer dared to attack the Prophet directly now. So they resorted to making life difficult for the weaker followers of the new religion.

The worst one among these adversaries was Abu Jahl. He scolded and slandered and threatened tradesmen to ruin their businesses, he ambushed Muhammad's friends and had them beaten up most cruelly. Not all the believers could permanently endure, or even watch, this kind of persecution. "Muhammad, please allow us to fight them!" they begged. "We have to start defending ourselves, or else they will never stop bothering us." The situation weighed heavily on Muhammad's mind, too, but an open fight would only lead to more violence and even more misery. So he told his friends one day, "Go to Abyssinia. You will find a Christian ruler there, who is well known for his righteousness. He believes in the same God as we do, and he will take care that you can live in peace and quiet."

Of course leaving their home country was not easy for these people, and parting with Muhammad ﷺ was especially difficult for them. With heavy hearts several families set out for the long journey to Abyssinia.

Among the emigrants there were also Ruqayyah, the Prophet's daughter, and her husband Uthman. They left Mecca at night so as not to be held back by the Quraysh. As fast as possible they tried to reach the port of Shuayba in order to continue their journey by ship from there.

When the Quraysh learned about the night time departure, they took up pursuit immediately. Yet they were not able to catch up with the fleeing families, because their ship had already cast off. For those who had stayed behind in Mecca, circumstances became more and more difficult. The most influential adversaries of the Muslims convened and drew up a document that said:

Muslims are only allowed to live in the gorge at the edge of Mecca!
Marriages with members of the outcast families are forbidden!
Nobody is allowed to sell anything to them or to buy anything from them!

These regulations were hung up at the Kaaba. By no means did all of the inhabitants of Mecca agree with this measure, but they did not dare to publicly trespass against these instructions. Not even Hamzah was able to prevent the boycott, the more so as the Prophet did not allow him to use any force. Food and other necessary items could therefore only be obtained in secret.
For over two years, the young Muslim community suffered from the boycott. The result was hunger and fatigue.
Meanwhile there were some Meccans who could not watch this state of affairs any longer. Many of them had relatives among the outcasts. Eventually a young man named Hisham was the first one to pluck up courage. Determined, he went to Zuhayr, another young man, whose mother was Atika, an aunt of the Prophet's. He said to him, "Zuhayr, how do you sleep at night knowing that your relatives are poor and deprived of their rights and hardly have the bare necessities for living?" "What can I do about it by myself?" Zuhayr asked. "Together we are two people!" Hisham replied. "We have to find others who support our cause," Zuhayr suggested. "The more people we are the better." So Hisham went to Mutim and asked him the same question he had asked Zuhayr before. The next morning, a group of young Meccans gathered in front of the Kaaba. Zuhayr rose to speak:

“Meccans,” he called out, “do we want to keep on watching our relatives from the tribe of Banu Hashim starve because they are not allowed to trade with us? How can you eat and sleep in the face of this injustice?! I am telling you: we are not going home until this boycott document is torn up!”

"We have never approved of this matter!" one of the other men said in agreement.
Abu Jahl, who had listened to all of this, got very angry. "That is out of the question!" he yelled furiously. "The document stays where it is!" But as he looked around he realised that the majority of people were against him.
When at last Mutim reached for the document, Abu Jahl could not do anything about it. The brave young man wanted to tear it up right away, but when he glanced at it, something odd attracted his attention. He paused in surprise and took a closer look at the boycott appeal: the sun and the termites had obliterated the original script almost completely. Just a few letters were left. These, however, were clearly visible: "In your name, o Allah…," Mutim spelled out. "Unbelievable," the young man marvelled. "This is indeed a miracle! A divine sign!"
Abu Jahl turned away in anger. "That is just some trickery!" he railed. However, from that day on, the oppressors' document was invalid.
And so, at long last, the Prophet's community could take part in social life again.

Abyssinia

In the Wise King's Realm

Lost in thought, the king of Abyssinia donned his robes. Some time ago, a group of emigrants from Mecca had asked for protection and shelter in his country. Apparently, there had been a number of serious conflicts in Mecca. The king did not know exactly what these quarrels had been about, but the Meccans were excitable just like his own people; sometimes an ill-chosen word was enough to provoke a bloody family feud. As king of Abyssinia, however, he had no reason to deny the immigrants from Mecca their request. Therefore, he offered them the same hospitality as he always used to.

A few hours ago, two emissaries from Mecca had appeared before his throne. They had brought gifts and asked for the immigrants' extradition, who – as the two Meccans had claimed – were agitators and runaway slaves. The kingdom of Abyssinia had always maintained good trade relations with the Meccans. The king did not want to put these relations at risk. However, he was not pleased with the two envoys' demeanour. First they had presented him with gifts, but then they had virtually demanded the people to be surrendered. Since the king had already granted the immigrants his hospitality, they were now under his personal protection. It was his duty to at least listen to what they had to say before he made a decision. So the king of Abyssinia reached for his sceptre and entered the adjacent room, where the spokesmen of the two parties were already waiting for him.

One of the envoys from Mecca stepped forward. "Master, these men are agitators!" he shouted. "They do not abide by the rules. Subversives, that's what they are! They incite our slaves. They listen to no one except their leader Muhammad. They are very likely to cause trouble here in Abyssinia soon, too. Believe me, Master; it's better for you to hand them over to us."

The king turned to the accused and said: "Well, you have heard the accusations addressed to you. What have you to say for yourself?"

"Honoured king," one of them began to speak, "the members of our faith community have been persecuted and insulted for months in Mecca. The situation has become worse and worse lately. Many of us have been assaulted and mistreated. One fellow believer's parents were tortured and killed. Our women and children were living in constant fear. We were not able to bear this any longer. So we decided to fight for our rights. However, when we told Muhammad about our intention, he advised us against it and said, "It is better for you to go to Abyssinia. There is a Christian king there. He believes

in God just as we do, and he is a just ruler. The king of Abyssinia will protect you. In his country you will certainly find life easier'."

"Honoured king", the spokesman continued, "this man accuses us of trespassing against the old order. But what order is that? In reality, what is ruling in Mecca is the law of inhumanity! It knows no justice and no mercy. But Muhammad teaches us to be kind, forgiving and helpful towards all people. This is what God wants from us, he says. He also explained to us that God created the woman as the man's companion and that she is just as valuable as a man. Muhammad instructed us to take in the orphans from the streets. We offer them homes now. He himself never goes to sleep before he has given out all the money in his bag to the poor. Muhammad teaches us the divine order! The law of love and mercy."

The king had been listening carefully. "Who is this Muhammad? How does he know what God expects from us?"

"God speaks to him," the young man explained with conviction. "Muhammad is a prophet. Through the Angel Jibril he receives revelations directly from God. Did Allah not speak to people through different prophets in former times, too? Why should he not do the same nowadays? After all, Abraham, Noah, Moses and Jesus were also sent by God to teach people. In all his life, Muhammad has never learned how to read and write, but the words he passes on to us are unique. They contain the truth – and besides they sound more beautiful than any poetry."

The king of Abyssinia grew more and more pensive. "The words of your Muhammad very much resemble those of Jesus Christ," he finally answered. "They are like two rays from the same lamp."
"Don't let yourself be fooled," one of the envoys called out furiously. "They say that Jesus was just an ordinary man, not the son of God!"
"He was a man indeed, but not an ordinary one!" one of the emigrants explained patiently. "There is a verse which describes how the Angel Jibril visits Virgin Mary and announces to her that she would give birth to a son. Jibril says to her, 'God sends me to announce to you the birth of a son.' She asked, 'How is this possible? No man has ever touched me.' 'And yet it will happen,' Jibril answered, 'for God creates whatever He wants. He says,

﴾ *He said: So it will be! Your Lord says: It is easy to Me.*
And We will make him a sign to the people
and a mercy from Us.
And it is a matter which has been decreed.' ﴿
(Surah 19, Verse 21)

"The difference between you and us is indeed no bigger than the length of this stick," the king decided. "You can go home!" he ordered the Quraysh envoys, "and tell those who sent you that these people here are under my personal protection. I would not hand them over to you for all the gold in the world. They shall be safe in my country for as long as they wish."

Umm Hani

Grief in the Family

Umm Hani put down a jug of fresh water in front of her. With delight she let a small amount of it run down her hands. Then she washed her face and arms and feet the way Muhammad ﷺ had shown them. She loved this refreshment just as much as she loved the prayer. Since she had got accustomed to this regular break in her daily routine, she could not imagine living without it anymore. She enjoyed these few moments of silence more than anything in the world. While she was praying, the thoughts and worries of the day took a backseat for a while. In this way she could regain new strength. Today she was especially looking forward to the prayer because her cousin Muhammad ﷺ had come for a visit. Her father, Abu Talib, had always treated him like his own son, and she and Muhammad ﷺ had grown up like brother and sister. Umm Hani loved Muhammad ﷺ like her own brother.

Since the boycott had been ended, many things had at first changed for the better in Mecca. The excluded families had returned to their former homes.

Umm Hani was glad that they all could lead their normal lives again. The house of Muhammad ﷺ and his wife Khadijah had constantly been full of guests of late. The news had spread like wildfire: "Allah has sent a new messenger and leader to the people! Muhammad ﷺ is the long-desired Prophet of God!"

A lot of people wanted to know what this new Prophet had to say. The visitors came from all regions of Arabia. Muhammad ﷺ made time for each one of them. He talked to them about God and gave them advice.

Khadijah had always been a generous hostess. Some of the guests brought along food or gifts, and so in spite of there being many people in the house there was always enough food for everyone. It almost looked as if the Muslims had overcome their hardest time – but very soon and within a short period two unfortunate events happened.

First, Abu Talib had died. His death had not come as a complete surprise; after all, Abu Talib had seen lots of moons rise in his life. And yet, Umm Hani missed her father a great deal. Apart from that, his death brought new problems for the Muslim community. Abu Talib had not only been the head of their family but also the chief of the entire Hashemite tribe. He had always tried to protect his foster son Muhammad ﷺ and his family. But now her father's brother, her uncle Abu Lahab, had been pronounced the new chief of the tribe.

Unfortunately, Abu Lahab was among the avowed adversaries of their religion. Umm Hani was quite certain that he would soon try to cause the Muslims trouble.

Just a few days after her father's bereavement, another death shook the family: all of a sudden, Muhammad's wife Khadijah died entirely unexpectedly. Umm Hani still could not believe that Khadijah was actually dead. She had always been so full of power and liveliness. The women of Mecca had asked Khadijah for advice in all matters. All her life she had been at the centre of society.

In his life, Muhammad ﷺ had often had to bid farewell to people he loved, but this time he was especially deeply heart-stricken. In addition, it grieved him to see his four daughters' pain; Fatima, Zaynab, Umm Kulthum and Ruqayya were overwhelmed by sorrow. Muhammad ﷺ tried everything to console them. He told them that the Angel Jibril had visited him once more before their mother's death. "Allah, our Lord, sends a greeting of peace to Khadijah!" the Angel had said. "Deliver this message to her and tell her also that a dwelling is ready for her in Paradise."

Khadijah's death may have been the reason why Muhammad ﷺ came to visit more often now. Perhaps the Prophet sometimes did not feel like going back to his own big house, where he had spent so many years together with his wife. Whatever might have been his motives, Umm Hani was glad about the Prophet honouring her and her family so often with his visit lately.

Umm Hani felt a slight draught of air cool her wet forehead. Refreshed, she set the water jug aside and closed its opening with a flat stone. Full of joy, she then went to meet the Prophet in order to perform the prayer together with him.

The Night Journey

The Wondrous Ride on the Buraq

Muhammad ﷺ finished the night prayer. Only now did he realise how tired he was. His cousin Umm Hani had invited him to stay overnight in her house, and since Muhammad ﷺ knew how happy Umm Hani was about his visits, he had gladly accepted the offer. He had had a hard day; it was not easy for him to get used to the fact that Khadijah was no longer with him. Muhammad's heart grew heavy every time he thought of her. Where there had been her warmth and laughter just a short while ago, there now was this indescribable emptiness. In the afternoon, on top of it all Abu Lahab had crossed his path, who, as usual, had tried to provoke him with his poisonous words. Most of the times, this did not bother Muhammad ﷺ too much, but at the moment he found it very hard to tolerate this additional strain. Umm Hani had tried everything to bolster him up, and her caring manner had done him good, yet he felt as exhausted as hardly ever before. So he thanked his cousin for her hospitality and retired to his bed. As soon as he lay down he fell asleep.

He was not to know that at the same moment the Angel Jibril was on his way to the Earth. Allah had told Jibril: "Clothe yourself in your best garments and go to Muhammad ﷺ, my dearest servant. When he fell asleep tonight he was so sad. He has to endure a lot for my sake. Therefore I will bestow a special honour on him tonight. I will show him things that no man has ever seen before him. Choose the most beautiful Buraq from Paradise and take it along for him to ride. Then bring him to me."

A few moments later, the Angel was standing beside Muhammad ﷺ, gently touching his shoulder. "Wake up, Muhammad," he said, "your Creator, who never sleeps, is calling you!" Muhammad ﷺ opened his eyes in surprise. Jibril handed him a jar that contained water from the

Paradise for him to wash himself. Astonished, Muhammad ﷺ washed with the heavenly water and followed the Angel outside. There, in the silence of the night, the most beautiful and extraordinary creature the Prophet had ever seen was expecting them. It was called a Buraq. The Buraq's body was white as snow and horse-like but its face was human, and on the back of the heavenly creature there was a majestic pair of wings. The Buraq was overjoyed to carry the Prophet on its back. As fast as a beam of light it soared into the night sky with Muhammad ﷺ. With every stride of its hooves it covered a huge distance, each stride reached the farthest point the Prophet could distinguish with his eyes. Soon Muhammad ﷺ could see the walls of the holy temple in Jerusalem below him. A group of prophets had gathered there who had lived on earth before Muhammad ﷺ. Among them were Abraham, Moses and also Jesus. The Buraq came to a stop near the walls and the Prophet tethered it to a ring where in earlier times other prophets had tied their mounts.

All the prophets that were present lined up behind Muhammad ﷺ for prayer. After the prayer Muhammad ﷺ was offered two earthen dishes, one of which was filled with milk, the other one with wine. The Prophet took the dish that contained the milk and drank it. The wine he did not touch. Jibril saw this and said to him, "You are walking on the right path and you are guiding others on the right path."

After this pause Muhammad ﷺ continued his journey. A gleaming ladder appeared in the night sky, on which Muhammad ﷺ, with Jibril at his side, climbed further up to heaven. The Buraq stayed in Jerusalem to take the Prophet back home safely from there later.

On their way, the Prophet and his companion passed by myriads of clouds and stars. Every time they got from one heaven to the next, Jibril asked for admittance. "Who is with you?" the angels asked every time.

Jibril replied, "It is Muhammad!", and the angels greeted the Prophet joyfully. "Welcome, welcome, honoured visitor!" they called. The earlier prophets, Abraham, Moses, Jesus and all the others had also returned from the prayer in Jerusalem to their heavenly abodes. "May God give you life, o brother and friend!" they exclaimed as soon as they saw Muhammad ﷺ.

Muhammad ﷺ got sight of the different paradises and their happy dwellers. Through the gates of these paradises, seven hundred thousand angels went in and out every day. Each centimetre of the paradises was infinitely more beautiful than the most miraculous places on earth. However, he also saw the gates of hell and the people in it.

A little later, Jibril and Muhammad ﷺ reached an ancient lotus tree. Behind its mighty crown was Allah's throne. "I have to take leave of you here now," Jibril said, "for from this point you have to go on alone."

Devoutly, Muhammad ﷺ walked the last few steps unaccompanied. Soon he got sight of the divine throne. Allah had created it from green emeralds with legs made of red ruby. A hundred thousand rows of angels were floating around the throne, singing unceasingly, "Praise and glory to our Creator!"

On the throne there was light over light. It was so bright that no creature had ever dared to look into it directly. At this moment, Muhammad ﷺ was cloaked by the divine light of love. His heart was enlightened by all the wisdom and all the knowledge of all things that had ever been and all things that were to happen in the future.

Muhammad ﷺ felt happiness flow through him. All the events that had burdened his life up to then just dissipated. He bathed in the divine light as if it was an infinite, shimmering ocean.

Abu Bakr

A Friend's Trust

Abu Bakr was sitting on the floor in the corner of the meeting room reflecting. He was worried about his friend Muhammad ﷺ Since Khadijah had died he had changed a great deal. Before that, Muhammad ﷺ had often smiled; he had taken pleasure in cheering up the people around him. In the last few weeks, though, Muhammad ﷺ himself had often seemed to be sad, even gloomy. On top of that, there was the spitefulness of Abu Jahl and his gang. Just a few days ago, they had thrown stones at Muhammad ﷺ again. Abu Bakr sighed. If only he could do something to help him!

There he was! Muhammad ﷺ came in and Abu Bakr leapt to his feet to greet him. Almost at the same time, Abu Jahl entered the room as well. In surprise, Abu Bakr noticed that the Prophet was still all smiles. His heart made a leap when Muhammad ﷺ greeted him with a smile. While the Prophet was greeting the others present, Abu Bakr went on watching him closely. He had the feeling that Muhammad ﷺ had something important to tell them today.

Abu Bakr was anxiously waiting for what the Prophet would say as soon as he had finished his prayer, when Abu Jahl shouted maliciously, "Now do tell people what you told me just now. We will see if there is even one person here who believes the story to be true that you wanted to make me believe."

At last, Muhammad ﷺ turned around and said, "Yesterday I performed my night prayer here in Mecca. Then I went to the holy temple in Jerusalem, where I performed another prayer. And then I said my morning prayer here in Mecca again." He told them about his journey to the ruins of the holy temple in Jerusalem. Abu Bakr listened to him in fascination. Only after Muhammad ﷺ had ended his account did Abu Bakr become aware of those around him again. Doubt was written in their faces. One of them stood up and said: "We would really like to believe you, but we have never heard such a story. Every child in Mecca knows that it takes a whole month for a caravan to travel to Jerusalem and another month to come back. How would you be able to make this journey in one single night?"

Looking annoyed, Abu Bakr shook his head. "Why do they not believe him?" he wondered, "Has Muhammad ever told a lie?" They still called him al-Amin, the Trustworthy, yet they did not trust him.
Abu Bakr did not have the slightest doubt that what Muhammad ﷺ had told them was true. "If he said it, then it is true!" Abu Bakr called

out aloud. "News from heaven reaches him within one single hour even. Isn't that much more astonishing?"
But people were still full of doubt. At last they asked the Prophet, "Don't you have any proof that what you say is true?"
Abu Bakr was astonished at Muhammad's patience. Friendly and composed as always he replied, "I can give you the proof." And Muhammad described the temple in Jerusalem in full detail to his listeners.

"The description is correct," a man from Jerusalem, who knew the building, confirmed. "This is exactly what the temple looks like." People knew that Muhammad ﷺ had never been in Jerusalem up to this time; yet they were not completely convinced.

"Besides, I met a caravan on my journey," Muhammad ﷺ continued. "The caravan had lost one of their camels." Muhammad ﷺ described to his listeners exactly where he had met the caravan, when it would most probably reach Mecca and the place where the camel had been found again.

Shortly afterwards this caravan actually arrived in Mecca, just as Muhammad ﷺ had predicted it. The men from the mosque asked the participants of the caravan about the camel that had been lost. Surprised, the travellers answered their questions. "How do you know about the escaped camel?" they asked puzzled. "We have only just arrived and have not told anyone about it yet."

At long last the listeners now began to believe the story of Muhammad's night journey. Abu Bakr sighed with relief. All too easily this issue could have got Muhammad ﷺ into difficulties again – of which he had more than enough.

A little while later, Abu Bakr heard about the last part of the journey as well, about Muhammad's ascension from Jerusalem through the heavens until high up to the presence of God. Finally Muhammad ﷺ also related that Allah had given the order to all believers to raise the number of daily prayers to five. "They should actually have been fifty prayers," the Prophet explained, "but on my way back through the heavens I met the Prophet Musa again. 'Welcome, my brother and friend,' he said to me, 'I'm very glad to see you again!' Then he asked me, 'Has Allah given you anything to take along to your community?' So I told Musa about the fifty prayers. He replied, 'Oh Muhammad, people are weak and their lives are short. It would be too great a burden on them to perform such a high number of prayers every day. Allah is gracious. I advise you to go back to Him and ask Him whether He could reduce the number.'

'My brother,' I replied, 'I've come all the way down through the heavens, I cannot simply go back again.' He replied, 'You can make your request just as well from here, for Allah is always near you, no matter where you are.'

So I followed his advice. Allah answered at once and reduced the number of prayers to forty-five. But in Musa's opinion this was still too much, so I made my request another time. And so it went on until in the end only five prayers were left. I had just decided not to ask any more when I heard Allah's voice say, "Muhammad, return to your people now. I have limited the number of the obligatory daily prayers to only five. One prayer shall count as ten prayers. Moreover, I will reward every good deed tenfold, but record every sin only once.'"

With fascination and deep emotion, Abu Bakr had listened to Muhammad's words. Yet he was glad that Muhammad ﷺ had confided this second part of the story only to his closest relatives and friends, for he feared more than ever for Muhammad's safety.

Even some of the believers had their doubts about Muhammad's words. Several of them came to Abu Bakr and asked him, "Do you really believe that all the things he says are right? Can it be true that he travelled to Jerusalem and from there to heaven until God's throne and back to Mecca – all in one night?"
"If he said it, then it is true," Abu Bakr replied. "And if Muhammad told me that he had travelled much farther and returned in the same night, I would still believe him. I would witness in front of every human being that he says nothing but the truth."
When the Prophet heard this, he gave his friend Abu Bakr the name "as-Siddiq", he who confirms the truth.

Abbas

The Pledge of Aqaba

Like every year at the same time, pilgrims from all parts of Arabia had set out to travel to Mecca and render homage to the idols at the Kaaba.

This year, a small group of Muslims from Yathrib, a flourishing oasis town just a few days' ride from Mecca, had unobtrusively joined the stream of people travelling there. However, the Muslims pursued their own plans…

As always, the festivities marking the end of the pilgrimage had been a lavish celebration. Now the various travel communities were camping in the Plains of Arafat. Cool moonshine had replaced the searing desert sun and immersed the rocky ground in silver-grey light. It was well into the night when in the camp of the pilgrims of Yathrib several persons rose soundlessly. Unnoticed by their sleeping clansmen, they crept to their camels, took them by the reins and led them away. A bit further away, they mounted the camels and trotted off.

At the same time, Muhammad ﷺ and his uncle Abbas were speedily riding from Mecca towards the rocky gorge of Aqaba. They arrived in the gorge at about the same time as the riders from the camp of the Khazraj.
In the dark one could heard the sound of the camels pawing the ground. The silhouettes of the arriving riders stood out against the rocks. Only a few rays of the silvery moonlight found their way into the gorge. After the eyes had got used to the sparse lighting, the riders dismounted. Only the white of their eyes flashed in the dark. Among those present there were also two women. Just like the men of their tribe they did not want to miss out on the opportunity to meet the Prophet himself. He was said to be an advocate for women and to give them special rights. Although they were not normally included in the plans and conversations of the men, the women had realised that important decisions were to be made today. Together with the men, they were eagerly expecting the meeting with the Prophet. Suddenly the slender silhouette of the Prophet appeared at the entranceway of the gorge, accompanied by Abbas, who – although not yet a Muslim – had promised to support the Prophet and defend his life, and so Abbas was vigilantly observing everything around him in order to be aware immediately of even the slightest sign of danger. With a protective gesture he planted himself next to his nephew, his hand at the hilt of this sword, ready to react as fast as lightning to protect the Prophet's life.

When all people present had exchanged their greetings, they sat down to talk. "Honoured Prophet," one of the Khazraj spokesmen said. "You know what it is like in our town of Yathrib. Tribesmen of the three tribes that live there – the Jews, the Khazraj and the Aws – have been fighting for supremacy for years on end. The hostility between them has grown more and more in the last few years. No solution is in sight; again and again this leads to people being injured and killed. It is dreadful! Everyone is suffering from this situation. Yet the people in our town are not willing to acknowledge a leader from one of the other tribes. Now Islam gives us new hope. Since your emissary Musab has been teaching your religion in Yathrib and reciting verses from the Qur'an, more and more people in our town are embracing the new faith. In this way, many have become brothers and sisters, regardless of which family they come from. They buried their enmity and live together in peace now. We have come tonight to put forward a proposal to you: in Mecca, you and your followers are in constant danger. With every step you take you all have to fear for your safety, and your enemies will not give you any peace in the future either.

In our town, however, in Yathrib, you and your followers would be welcome. People are longing for peace, which you could give them. They are tired of fighting. In our town you could really accomplish something great. You are the best leader of all, and they would accept you because you are a foreigner. In this way, none of our men would lose his face. At the same time, your community would be out of harm's way. We beg you to honour our town with your presence and come to live with us!"

The people present were immersed in a tense silence. The informers of the Quraysh had already found out that the Prophet had been in contact with the people of Yathrib for some time, a fact that was a thorn in the flesh of Muhammad's enemies. Full of wrath they had realised that the Prophet's influence was increasing more and more in this place as well. It was as clear as glass that they would not watch idly as things went on. There had even been rumours in Mecca lately about a plan of a murderous attack on the messenger of God...

Abbas rose to speak to them. "My nephew has already resolved to join you. You know what he means to us. In Mecca he has a lot of enemies, but I myself and many others are prepared to defend him – with our own lives, if need be. If Muhammad goes with you, it will be your duty to protect him. Are you sure that you want to take this responsibility and that you are prepared to give your lives if necessary? If deep down in your hearts you have doubts and fear that you might betray him in such a situation, then you had better make up your minds now and go home before it is too late."

At that the Prophet rose and recited some verses from the Qur'an. Then he said, "I saw your city in a dream. If you agree to make a pledge with me, I will go with you. Are you willing to vow to protect me just as you would protect your own families?"

After these words, a man named Bara rose and said, "In the name of Allah the Merciful Who sent you, we will protect you like we protect our own relatives. We have been skilled fighters for many generations and will be faithful to you and serve you under all circumstances. But if we do so, we have to dissolve our old alliances. If God helps you to prevail over your enemies, then who can guarantee us that you are not going to leave us and return to your own people? If this were the case, we would be left with nothing as we would no longer have our present allies either."

"Do not worry," the Prophet smiled. "This will never happen. I belong to you just as you belong to me. I will fight against whoever fights you, and whoever you form a friendship with I will also have peace with. And I promise you that each one of you who fulfils his oath will enter Paradise."

In order to set the seal on his words, he extended his hand to each of the men. In return, he received the oath of allegiance from all people present. The women also promised their devotion to Islam and its Prophet. However, the Prophet did not ask them to promise to fight if there was need.

Happy about the outcome of the negotiation and full of hope for a better future, the new allies bade each other farewell.

When shortly after that the Prophet was riding back with his uncle Abbas and could already see the outlines of Mecca, the vision of his dream once more formed before his inner eye for a moment:

A fertile land, rich in water, situated in an area of black rocks. Above the fields of the oasis, the vibrant green of date palms softly swaying in the wind...

Yes! Allah himself had shown him the way to Yathrib with this dream! A good place to make a new start! As soon as possible he would send his companions there and then set out for Yathrib himself.

Ali

The Deception

Ali curled up under his coat. Even though it was well into the night, he was lying on his bed wide awake. At every little noise he held his breath. Wasn't there a rustle outside the door? Wasn't something moving out there? Ali knew that at least a dozen men were sneaking around in the dark outside, armed to the teeth and ready to kill. "Why haven't they tried to enter the house by now?" Ali wondered. Whatever were they waiting for?

Ali knew that the men out there were not coming for him but for Muhammad ﷺ. Their anger and their fear of the Prophet's influence had grown sky high within the last few weeks and months. Now, in the very last moment, they wanted to prevent him from emigrating to Yathrib. They knew that Muhammad ﷺ was extremely popular with the inhabitants of that town. All Yathrib seemed to be waiting for his arrival. The tribal chieftains of Mecca were afraid that the Prophet might find even more followers there. In this case, they themselves might soon be greatly outnumbered. Thus they had decided to kill him. All of them together they would do it, viciously and insidiously, so that no one could tell which of them had actually committed the murder. Ali shook in disgust. He hoped that Muhammad ﷺ and Abu Bakr had gone far by now with their camels. The men were supposed to think that the Prophet was still lying in bed and sleeping, covered by his green coat. Ali held his breath. Wasn't there some noise again? He almost wished they would come at last and put an end to this insufferable suspense. But Ali knew that every second of advantage was of vital importance for Muhammad ﷺ and Abu Bakr. So he tried to stay calm and lay there as motionless as possible. Would they try to kill him when they realised that it was him and not the Prophet who was lying in bed under his coat? Ali could feel the dark presence of the men through the walls. But Muhammad ﷺ had said, "In my house there are still objects of value that people entrusted to my care. I cannot just leave these things behind. Please, Ali, stay in my house for a while until each of the owners has got their things back. Then follow me to Medina. Sleep in my bed and cover yourself with my coat. Do not worry, nothing will happen to you!" Before he left, the Prophet had recited a divine verse. He did that sometimes as a protection against looming disaster and danger. Yet, Ali spent the rest of the night vigilantly, hidden under the Prophet's green coat. He lay there, listening and praying, until dawn replaced the night. Then he could not bear it any longer. Had his pursuers perhaps given up their plan? Or discovered the imposture somehow? Ali took the coat, wrapped

himself in it and opened the door to leave the house. In this moment, hell broke loose around him. From all sides Abu Jahl's men lunged at him. Ali realised too late that all along they had been waiting for the moment when Muhammad ﷺ usually left the house in the morning. He was going to die! "Over and done," Ali thought. At this moment, one of the men shouted, "Stop it! Stop! It's not him! It's Ali! Don't you see that this is Ali?"
Ali felt brutal hands tear down the coat. A moment later he looked into the perplexed faces of several men. It took a moment before they had realised that they had been deceived. They let go of Ali. Seconds later he was standing there alone in the dawn. "Oh Allah," he prayed, "I beg You to protect Your Prophet from these people."

The Cave

A Hideout for the Prophet and his Friend

Before nightfall, Abu Bakr had already begun to make preparations for the departure. Two sturdy camels were ready and waiting for their riders. Moreover, Abu Bakr had called his daughter Asma and given her a few instructions: "Muhammad and I will probably spend the next three days and nights in a cave," he had explained to her. "It is not too far from here, at the mountain of Thawr. You know the place. I want you to bring us food there every night."

And he told his son Abdullah, "The Quraysh will soon pursue us and try to find us. Observe them and make a report to us about where they are."

Shortly after midnight the two men set out. Darkness engulfed the lonely riders like a protective cloak. No one was watching their departure except for Amir, the shepherd, a former slave who had been bought and set free by Abu Bakr. He had offered to cover the two men's tracks by driving his flock across them.

The next morning, the pursuers noticed to their surprise that the Prophet had already left town.

Meanwhile, Muhammad ﷺ and Abu Bakr had long reached the entrance of the cave.

Exhausted, they settled into their rocky shelter. The Prophet closed his eyes for a moment, his head resting on Abu Bakr's knee. How good it was to have a friend in these difficult moments! Abu Bakr was too tense to sleep.

Meanwhile in Mecca, Muhammad's pursuers had gathered in front of Abu Bakr's house. They had knocked at the door and asked for Asma. When Asma came to the door, one of the men called, "Where did they go, your father and Muhammad? You are certainly well informed!" But Asma pretended to be surprised and replied, "I do not know." Abu Jahl made a threatening step towards her. Then he raised his hand and gave Asma a slap on the ear, so that one of her earrings fell in the sand. Appalled, Asma stared at the man and backed off. Her cheek was burning, but she did not say a word. Finally the men trudged away impatiently.

In the evening she secretly sneaked off to the cave, intent on bringing food to her father and to Muhammad ﷺ and to report to them what had happened.

The men were still searching in the wrong direction. However, it was only a question of time before they would remember the abandoned cave, because the people of Quraysh were familiar with every square inch of the surrounding area.

After just a few days, Abu Bakr heard muted voices outside the cave. He strained his ears, trying to recognise some of the voices. His heart was pounding like mad. The Prophet noticed his friend's agitation. He looked at him reassuringly. "Allah will protect us," he whispered softly. "Don't worry."

Footsteps were approaching outside. Stones were scrunching. Abu Bakr and Muhammad ﷺ were praying silently for Allah's help. All of a sudden, they could understand the words that were spoken outside. "They cannot be here," one of them said. "Just look at the spider webs in front of the entrance – they are very old. For sure no one has entered here lately." "And look there ahead, there is even a pigeon breeding in its nest," another one called. "No, this area is completely

deserted. Let us go back. We are only wasting our time here." With these words, the riders turned their camels around and dashed away.
A little later, Muhammad ﷺ and Abu Bakr were marvelling at the huge web with the spider in its centre and at the nest with the breeding pigeon. "The animals have protected us," Abu Bakr stated with emotion in his voice. "When we came, all this was not here."
Shortly afterwards, the two friends left the cave to go on. They set out to Yathrib where they were eagerly expected. Soon after the Prophet's arrival, this town was named *al-Madinatu l-Munawwara*, the "Illuminated City" – or just: Medina.

Abu Ayyub

Entering Medina

All Medina was astir. Abu Ayyub was standing in the middle of the crowd, trying to catch a glimpse of the Prophet. The air was vibrating from the men's shouts of welcome. "Allahu akbar! God is most great!" they called. The women and children were cheering, and some of them began to sing:

"Tala'a l-badru 'alayna	*Oh the white moon rose over us*
Min thaniyati l-wada'	*From the valley of al-Wada'*
Wadjaba sh-shukru 'alayna	*And we owe it to show gratefulness*
Ma da'a li-llahi da'	*Where the call is to Allah.*
Ayyuha l-mab'uthu fina	*Oh you who were raised amongst us*
Dji'ta bi-l-amri l-muta'	*Coming with a word to be obeyed*
Dji'ta sharrafta l-madina	*You have brought to this city nobleness*
Marhaban ya khayra da'."	*Welcome best caller to God's way.*

Calmly the Prophet's she-camel Qaswa cleaved her way through the cheering multitude. The people of Medina were crowding around the Prophet's camel; everyone wanted to invite Muhammad ﷺ to come to their house. Some even grabbed the camel's reins to make the Prophet come with them. But Muhammad ﷺ said, "Let go of my camel, she knows where to go. Wherever she kneels down I will take a rest." "He is very polite indeed," Abu Ayyub thought, "and does not want to offend anyone. Oh, I wish the camel knelt down in front of our house!" he sighed wistfully.

Abu Ayyub and his wife were anxiously watching every step the camel took. Many people had placed buckets of water and feeding troughs in front of their doors to induce the animal to stop, but the camel would not be swayed. Then she finally stopped in front of one of the houses and knelt down. Abu Ayyub did not believe his eyes: it was really in front of his own house where the camel had knelt down. He quickly ran towards his house to welcome the Prophet and Abu Bakr. Muhammad ﷺ dismounted, greeted him and said, "Here, God willing, we will dwell."

Overjoyed, Abu Ayyub opened the door to usher the Prophet in. In doing so he noticed that a date palm grove nearby had caught Muhammad's eye. "Do you know who owns this ground?" the Prophet enquired.

"It belongs to two orphans named Sahl and Suhayl," Abu Ayyub explained. "The two boys are under my protection. If you would like

to have the grove, I will compensate them for it. I will make them an offer they are surely going to be satisfied with.
The Prophet asked his host to send for the two orphans. When they had come he said to them, "I would like to buy this ground from you. If you agree to sell it, think about how much it is worth to you and name a price." The two orphans looked at each other, thinking the same thing, and immediately replied, "Messenger of God, take it

as a present from us!" But the Prophet did not want to accept this. He insisted on paying the two generous orphans an appropriate amount of money for the piece of land. And so, with Abu Ayyub's help, they settled on a price in the end.

In this date palm grove, very soon work began to build the first mosque.

Aisha

The Beginning of New Times

At last Aisha could move to Medina together with her mother! Several months had passed since her father, Abu Bakr, had left in the middle of the night to flee to Medina with Muhammad ﷺ. Up to that time, there had never been a day – as long as she could remember – when the Prophet had not visited her family.

Aisha did not know anyone who was friendlier and kinder than Muhammad ﷺ. It was a complete mystery to her why there were people in Mecca who disliked him. For years on end they had pursued and oppressed him, with his own uncle Abu Lahab leading the way. In the end they had even tried to murder him, and so he had had no other choice but to secretly leave the city under cover of darkness.

Aisha knew that Muhammad ﷺ was the Messenger of God. On his visits he often told them about his encounters with Jibril. Aisha loved to hear the Prophet talk about the mighty angel. She never got enough of it. There was no keener listener than Aisha. Besides, she had a good memory and therefore was capable of memorising each detail of his accounts. Aisha took great interest in them and she knew that Muhammad ﷺ was particularly happy about this.

One day she would marry the Prophet, she already knew that, because to him an angel had appeared in a dream, with a silken cloth in his hands. The angel had pointed to the cloth and said, "This is your wife". Muhammad ﷺ had uncovered the cloth and found her, Aisha, in it.

Other young girls might dream about marrying a rich Bedouin prince, but her heart was beating for Muhammad ﷺ only. A smile from him meant more to her than anything else, and the fact that he was so much older than her did not matter to her.

Neither did the fact that he had recently married the widow Sawda change her feelings. In Mecca it was quite possible for a man to have more than one wife. Often there was no other way, for if a man died for some reason, it was next to impossible for the widow to feed herself and her children on her own. These women were glad if another family took them in, for in this way they were provided for. Naturally, there were often conflicts between the wives, but in most cases they lived together quite well. Aisha knew how much work there was in a household. Families in Mecca were big, so sometimes it was better if it was not only one woman who had to do all the work alone.

Besides, Sawda was quite old already, and Aisha was young and pretty.

She liked the older woman and knew that Sawda liked her too. Apart from that, there was nothing to do about the fact that the Prophet was already married to Sawda. Even so she did not want to marry any other man.

In excitement Aisha packed her few belongings. She did not feel sorry about leaving Mecca. Her parents and siblings would be with her, and also her family were not the only ones who decided to follow the Prophet to Medina. A major part of her closest friends and relatives were also busy preparing their departure for Medina.

When Aisha arrived there a few days later, several things had already changed in Medina. The Prophet had bought the ground next to Abu Ayyub's house and had decided to build a mosque there. It was almost finished. At the eastern wall of the building two houses had been attached: one house for Sawda and one for Aisha.

Aisha heard the men sing while they were building the mosque. Muhammad ﷺ had also worked together with them most of the time in the past few weeks. Suddenly the singing was interrupted by a powerful voice. The men put down their tools and stood up. It was the first time they heard the call.

"Allahu akbar, Allahu akbar!" the voice sounded. "God is great, God is great!" And once again, "Allahu akbar, Allahu akbar! Ashadu an la ilaha illallah, ashadu anna Muhammadan rasoolullah…," it resounded. "I bear witness that there is no deity but God and that Muhammad is his Prophet…"

It was Bilal, the former slave, who was standing on the roof of a nearby house, calling people for prayer in a loud voice from there. Suddenly people came from all directions who wanted to go to the mosque.

Aisha saw the believers line up in many lines for prayer. "Here in Medina, new times will begin for all of us," she thought happily.

Medina

City of the Prophet

Among the inhabitants of Medina there were two tribes that had been on bad terms with each other for a long time. The local Jews had also taken sides. Now everyone was hoping that these conflicts would be settled.

Muhammad ﷺ was appointed the new head of the city of Medina. He wanted all people in Medina to live their lives in peace, security and justice. Under his rule, an entirely new order developed. No one in Medina could be pursued or banished for his creed. Women were allowed to inherit, to act as witnesses and to conclude marriage contracts in order to secure their rights. Slaying newborn girls was declared a serious crime and made a punishable offence with harsh penalties. Muhammad ﷺ also decreed that Muslims had to give a fixed proportion of their wealth to the poor. The aim of this alms giving, or zakat, was that no one should go hungry or be compelled by poverty to steal.

"None of you can be considered a believer if he eats until he is full while his neighbour is hungry", the Prophet reminded again and again.

One day a young man from Medina came to the Prophet and said, "I can see how good and just your laws are, but I cannot pay zakat or make donations. I have just enough to get by. But I would really like to make a beneficent contribution too. What can I do?" Muhammad ﷺ replied, "You can give your alms in another way: helping a man mount his horse or camel and carrying his baggage is also a valuable deed. Answering a question with patience and lenience or creating justice between people is also an important contribution to community. You can help by removing things that can cause an inconvenience to other people, like thorns or stones; this is also a beneficent deed. Even giving someone a smile is a kind of charity."

The holy month of Ramadan was declared a fasting month. From now on, for all Muslims fasting began at the time of the Morning Prayer shortly before sunrise every day and ended in the evening at sunset. During this time of fasting nobody ate or drank. Instead, people devoted themselves to inner reflection and prayer. In the evenings, the Prophet had food distributed to all people who were hungry and came to his house.

Within a very short time, word got around all over Arabia about the enormous changes that were going on in Medina. All kinds of stories about the Prophet were circulating. Above all, everywhere people spoke about his limitless generosity.

One day, a man set out to Medina to meet Muhammad ﷺ. He said to him, "I have heard that you are the most generous of all people. I am poor and can hardly feed my family any more. Could I ask you for a couple of sheep?" Quite near, between two hills, a great number of Muhammad's sheep was grazing. The Prophet gave the man all the sheep.

When the man returned to his village with the animals, he said, "I've never experienced anything like this. No one has a heart as big as Muhammad's. He actually gives away everything he owns and yet he is not at all afraid of becoming poor."

Umar

Preparations for the Attack

Umar was observing the contours of the dunes attentively. Nothing was moving in the distance. Only rarely was the silence around him interrupted by the hoarse lowing of a camel or by scraps of conversations blown over to Umar from the men's camp.

Not long ago, the Prophet had received a message which said that the Meccans were now planning to attack Medina. They did not even shy away from that! It had long been Umar's opinion that it was time to put those trouble makers in their place.

Despite the positive developments in Medina he had not forgotten the circumstances that had forced them to emigrate: all the humiliation the Prophet had been exposed to. In the end they had tried to kill him. And the countless cruelties and acts of violence the believers had had to put up with. For years on end, the Muslims had endured all this, and there had even been fatalities. And when they emigrated, the families had to leave almost their entire possessions behind in

Mecca. Houses, shops, goods and tools, everything had fallen into the hands of the Quraysh. Thus many of the companions felt like guests in Medina rather than at home. Some of them had long been very eager to recapture everything they once had owned.

Muhammad ﷺ, however, had done everything he could to avoid violent conflict. He detested war and strictly forbade the believers to fight their pursuers. But the terrifying news about what was going on in Mecca once again proved that the Meccans were not willing to abandon their plans of attacking the community.

﴿ *Permission has been given to those who are being fought,*
Because they were wronged.
And indeed, Allah is well able to assist them.
Those who have been expelled from their homes without a just cause
Except that they say:
"Our Lord is Allah." ﴾
(Surah 22, Verse 39/40)

Since then, the companions had tried to ambush the caravans of the Quraysh several times, but unfortunately they had not been very successful. Umar thought, however, that on this day it would be different. They were absolutely determined to reclaim at least part of their belongings. But above all they had to face the attack on Medina.

Abu Sufyan, a declared enemy of the Prophet's, was on his way home from Syria to Mecca at that time, with a big caravan and part of the stolen goods. He had already sold a big amount of the booty and done good business in this way.

The distance from Syria to Mecca was long. Therefore, caravans usually broke their journey at the wells of Badr. There they rested, watered their animals and refilled their water skins.

Umar and the other men had been camping near these wells for quite a while. They had sent out scouts to look out for the caravan. Up until now, though, there was no news as to that. Umar's gaze fell upon the men gathered around him. There were Hamzah, Ali, Abu Bakr, Ubayda, Awf and Sawad. Sawad was virtually a boy still; despite

that he had wanted to come along. Others had followed the Prophet's call, too. Only Uthman, one of their strongest fighters, had stayed in Medina. His wife Ruqayya, the Prophet's daughter, had suddenly fallen seriously ill; it was possible that she was going to die. Umar's gaze came to rest on Muhammad ﷺ. He knew how hard it had been for him to leave his daughter behind sick like this. But as always he put his own concerns aside if it was necessary for the community. Like all the others who were gathered here, Umar, too, would have given his life for the Prophet without hesitation. Nevertheless, he could not comprehend why Muhammad ﷺ did not take a tougher stance sometimes.

"If it had been up to me, we would have put up a fight against the Quraysh much earlier," Umar thought. "It's bad enough that it has come to this." Lost in thought, he watched a lizard disappear between the yellow tufts of tough grass. When he raised his eyes again, he spotted the shape of two horsemen on the ridge of a dune. They were the scouts. "Abu Sufyan has changed his route," they reported, "and he is already on his way to Mecca. Also, we have sighted about a thousand armed men who are riding from Mecca towards the caravan to protect it."

Umar leapt to his feet. Apparently Abu Sufyan had been warned. All the same, he had no intention of going back home without having achieved anything. He would not abandon this matter so easily.

A little later, Muhammad ﷺ gathered the men around him and asked them to give their opinion on the new situation. "Among the attackers there will be relatives of ours," Abu Bakr pointed out, "but whatever your decision will be, we will follow your order." At that, Umar called, "Let us no longer avoid them, brothers! As long as at least one of us is alive, we should fight."

Umar wasn't alone with this opinion. Hamzah and the other men no longer wanted to back down either. The time had come to face the Quraysh.

The Wells of Badr

An Unequal Fight

In the camp of the Quraysh, there were discussions of a similar kind at the same time. Utba, one of the more prudent among the Quraysh, made one more attempt to bring his men to reason: "In this war there will be no winners. Even if you defeat Muhammad and his companions, you will not be able to look at each other's faces later on. Those men over there are your relatives. After the fight you will hate each other for having killed each other's uncles and cousins."

At that, Abu Jahl berated Utba, calling him a coward. "You are only afraid for your own son who is sitting over there with Muhammad's people."

And so in the end, in this camp there were also more voices speaking in favour of war.

While Abu Sufyan's caravan arrived in Mecca unharmed, the army of the Quraysh got prepared to move towards Badr. They assumed that they would encounter the Prophet's followers there. A few days ago, one of the caravan's scouts had found fresh camel dung there which contained remains of date kernels. As he knew that this kind of feed was used in Medina, the scout had concluded that the riders of the army of Medina were camping at the wells of Badr. Thus the scout had been able to warn the caravan leaders early. The Meccan tribes had joined forces right away in order to defend the caravan and its precious load. Meanwhile the caravan was safe; however, the men had decided to fight anyway. Since the Medinans had appointed Muhammad ﷺ as the ruler of their city, he had been gaining more and more influence. The fact that he now began to ambush them made the Quraysh all the more furious.

The Quraysh started to move forward. A while later the fighters of the two hostile armies were facing each other. When the Meccans saw how small the number of their adversaries was they cheered, sure of victory. Muhammad ﷺ realised that the number of Meccans exceeded that of his own men many times over. Worried, he stood aside, asking God for assistance. "Allah, help us," he begged, "You know what lies ahead of us. I beg You, do not leave us without Your help today!"

A little later, he said to Abu Bakr, "Do not worry, Jibril is here! We will be victorious." Muhammad ﷺ knew that they depended on divine help, and Allah had promised to him, "I will help you with a thousand angels."

Then the battle began. The believers could feel the presence of the angels as a great force. Some even thought they had seen the angels for a moment, galloping through the air on heavenly horses.

The Quraysh, however, were horror-struck. A nameless fear took possession of them.

Thus the Quraysh were defeated in the end, in spite of their superior numbers. Most of them, however, were able to escape. About fifty of the Quraysh had been killed during the battle, among them Abu Jahl. The remaining combatants were taken captives by Muhammad's followers. They themselves had lost fourteen men.

"We should kill the captives right away!" Umar shouted, "They are wicked and only have bad intentions!" Muhammad ﷺ, however, rejected this practice. Jibril had instructed him to say the following to the men:

﴾ *O Prophet, say to those of the captives who are in your hands:*
"If Allah knows anything good in your hearts,
He will give you something better than
What was taken from you, and He will forgive you.
And Allah is Forgiving and Merciful." ﴿
(Surah 8, Verse 70)

Thus all combatants were ransomed by and by and could return to Mecca.

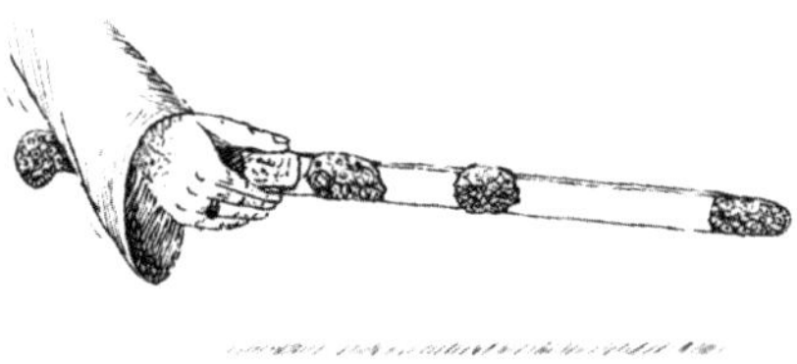

Fatima

The Modest Dowry

Tears were burning in Fatima's eyes. She stared down on the fresh grave mound made of soil and rocks. Just a few days ago, her sister Ruqayya had been buried here; she had not survived her illness. Fatima knew that she and her family were not the only ones who were in mourning these days. During the fighting at Badr, a lot of men from Medina had been killed. Thanks be to Allah – her own father Muhammad ﷺ had returned safely. Within just a few days, Muhammad ﷺ had had to bury not only his daughter but also some of his closest companions. Today again Fatima could hear a soft sobbing coming from a hut nearby. Parents were weeping for their sons, wives for their husbands and children for their fathers.

Fatima had great doubts that this war had ended. Certainly the Quraysh would soon try to take revenge for their losses. Then there would be even more dead people and more tears. If only there could be peace at last.

When Fatima went to sleep that night, she had no idea that not far from the mosque, in a hut almost like hers, young Ali was dreaming of his wedding. The beautiful bride in his dream was Fatima. Ali had loved Fatima for a long time. He would have liked to comfort her; but Ali did not dare to show her that he loved her or to ask her father for her hand. After all, Fatima was the Prophet's daughter. And he? What could he offer to her? The only thing he owned was the little hut he lived in. As Ali was dwelling on thoughts like these, he in turn had no idea that in the same night he was spoken about in the Prophet's bedroom.

The next day, Muhammad ﷺ summoned his daughter and Ali. When Fatima entered the room, the Prophet stood up and hugged her happily. To her surprise, Fatima noticed that Ali had been called to this meeting as well. Their eyes met shortly in greeting. She knew that Ali was one of her father's bravest and most faithful friends. She would never forget that Ali, without any hesitation, had lain down in her father's bed in his stead that night when Abu Jahl and his gang had planned to kill her father.

The Prophet gave Ali and Fatima an encouraging smile. "Sit down with me," he asked them. Then he told them about what happened the night before: Jibril had visited him again to disclose something important to him:

"Allah the Almighty has decreed a union in heaven between two young people: your daughter Fatima and Ali," Jibril had declared in a powerful voice. "Now let the two of them celebrate their wedding in this world, too."

Ali's heart began to beat wildly. He could not believe his luck: Allah had really chosen him for the Prophet's daughter! But would Fatima give her consent?

Lately there had not been much cause for joy. But now Fatima was smiling happily. Deep in her heart she, too, felt that Ali was the right man for her. Without hesitation she consented.

However, when a while later her father asked her, "What do you want me to give you as a dowry for your new household?" she grew thoughtful. Fatima was aware that people in Medina were always observing carefully what was going on in the Prophet's family. There were several reasons for that. Some people were just curious, but many people felt a strong attachment with her family. Her wedding would set an example for the citizens of Medina. So she answered, "If I asked you for money or gold, then how would the Prophet's daughter be different from other young women? I would rather support the girls who are poor. When a young woman gets married, her future parents-in-law ask her, 'How great is the fortune you bring into the marriage?' Then she is ashamed if she is poor and does not know what to answer. At the most she can say, 'My father was a good man. He brought me up to be friendly, kind, content and generous. These are the qualities I bring with me.'

I want every girl to base herself on me from now on; she can say, 'Even Fatima, our Prophet Muhammad's daughter, had no more than a handful of things as a dowry!'"

And that is how it came that Fatima brought just a few things to the new household, among them a pillow filled with palm fibre, a water skin, two cups and a woven basket. In spite of this, her wedding was one of the most beautiful and happiest weddings that had ever been celebrated in Medina.

The Defeat

Fatal Disobedience

As Fatima had feared, the battle of Badr was only the beginning of a war that was to last several years. Soon after Fatima and Ali's wedding the Angel Jibril appeared to warn the Prophet against the latest scheming of the Quraysh.

In fact, the Meccans had begun to set up a new army. This time, Abu Sufyan had taken command. Since he was one of the richest men in Mecca, he promised everyone who was willing to join his campaign fifty gold pieces as a reward. So it did not take long until he had put together a huge army of heavily armed fighters. These men were now getting prepared to go to Medina to fight the believers once again.

Canny as he was, Abu Sufyan had asked the women of Mecca to accompany their husbands in the campaign to "cheer them on during the fight", as he said. When women were near, Abu Sufyan was sure that the men would not show any cowardly behaviour. The group of women was headed by Abu Sufyan's wife Hind. Hind's father, Utba, had been killed in the battle of Badr. Since then, her hatred towards the believers had gone sky high. "We swear we will drink our enemies' blood!" she shouted again and again.

The situation being as it was, the Prophet mustered an army of volunteers. He intended to stay in Medina with the army and to defend the city from there if necessary. His men, however, were absolutely convinced that it was better to face the Meccan army in a different place; in the end he yielded. Thus the companions went to the foot of the mountain of Uhud to fight.

The Meccans took up position there as well. Abu Sufyan commanded most of his men; Khalid, the second commander, led the horsemen. The women were walking beside the men with their drums and were singing, "Our fighters will take revenge for the dead of Badr! Revenge for the dead of Badr!"

Now the Muslim lines were forming up for the battle. At some distance, Muhammad ﷺ had fifty archers take position on a hill. From there he would be able to overlook the war zone. "Wait here!" he impressed on them. "Do not leave this position for any reason."

Soon a fierce battle flared up between the two parties. The archers started to shoot their arrows against the Meccan cavalry as soon as they tried to approach. In the thick of the fray, Hamzah was grimly fighting like a lion against the superiority of their enemies. Hind was watching him. Shortly before the battle, she had promised her slave Wahshi a special reward if he succeeded in killing Hamzah. Wahshi was a trained spear thrower. With huge exertion of force he pitched the spear towards Hamzah. This blow hit him fatally. When Hind saw that Hamzah had been killed, she rushed across the battle field until she had found him. Heady with victory, she tore the liver out of the dead man's body to drink his blood from it as she had sworn.

At last the Prophet's followers succeeded in driving the Meccans back. From their position on the hill, the archers were watching some of their companions reach the enemy camp. At this moment they thought the battle was already won and the enemies were on the run, so they broke into cheers and forgot Muhammad's order

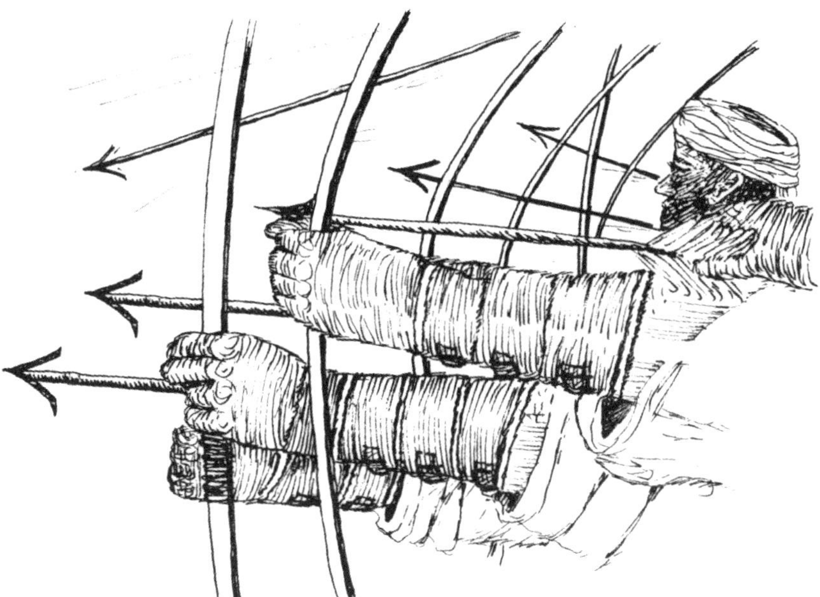

because they were afraid to be overlooked when the spoils were divided. "Let's go and get our share!" they shouted and ran down the hill into the valley. Khalid, the second commander, had only been waiting for such an opportunity. At once he took the abandoned hill with his horsemen. Now he could attack the Muslims from behind unopposed.

The defeat of the Muslim army was sealed. The stroke of a sword benumbed the Prophet. He fell down on the ground, blood streaming over his face. One of Abu Jahl's fighters had watched the stroke and shouted, "The Prophet is dead!" The Meccans started to cheer. The victory was theirs. The Muslims withdrew in shock.

Umar was the only one to realise that Muhammad ﷺ was still alive. The Prophet rose, swaying, to look for a safe place to go with the companions that were left. On coming closer, the Muslims recognised their Prophet. "He is alive! The Prophet is alive!" they rejoiced. The Quraysh heard these calls at the other end of the valley. "What is going on there?" they wondered. "Is it possible that Muhammad is not dead after all?"

The battle was over though. When darkness fell, countless Muslims had lost their lives. Muhammad ﷺ tried to comfort his companions assuring them, "Allah will give each one of them a place in Paradise."

Salman the Persian

With Shovel and Hoe

With a determined look on his face, Salman the Persian set out to the council meeting. Just a few minutes ago the Prophet himself had announced the news from Mecca: "Abu Sufyan and his army are on his way to Medina to attack us again. We have to get prepared. Do not be afraid – with Allah's help we will defeat them."

"He has united as many as 10,000 warriors!" the horsemen from Mecca had breathlessly informed him a short while before. "Among them there are some Bedouin tribes and also the Banu Nadir. The Quraysh alone make up about 300 horsemen, besides they have around 1,500 camels at hand. It is an enormous army, and it is easily three times as big as the one that defeated us at Uhud. They are a terrifying sight."

Salman shook his head in disgust. The Banu Nadir, a Jewish tribe, had conspired against the Prophet before. Muhammad ﷺ had shown leniency when the perpetrators were caught. Now the Nadir had formed an alliance with the Quraysh and the other tribes. Luckily, the Jewish families in Medina sided with the Prophet, who granted them all the rights the believing Muslims were entitled to.

Deep in thought, strong Salman did not even notice the expectant gazes that followed him while he was striding across the square. For the people of Medina, brave men like him were the hope bearers on this day.

When Salman entered the meeting room, his gaze immediately fell upon the Prophet, who was sitting amidst his closest companions. "We have about one week's time," Muhammad ﷺ was saying. "Would anyone like to make a suggestion as to how we should go ahead?" In the face of the anticipated superiority in numbers, all the suggestions that followed were discouraging.

"If I might say something...," Salman began. "As you know I am from Persia. There people have an efficient strategy by which one can stand a siege and stop the cavalry." The men looked across at Salman in amazement.

"We have to dig a trench," he continued. "A trench as wide and as deep as possible. They will have to stop in front of it. As soon as they move into the trench, they will be easy prey for our archers."

Surprised, the companions looked at each other. Of course! This plan sounded as if it could work. "This is how we will do it!" they decided enthusiastically, and Salman's suggestion was adopted unanimously.

Together Muhammad ﷺ and Salman marked the exact route of the trench and also its width and depth. Then the Prophet assigned certain sections of the trench to his men, where they set to work right away with shovels and hoes. Time was short, and so each one of them was working to the point of exhaustion.

Salman let his hoe crash down. Rocks, sand and soil came off under the hammering blows. He was used to hard work. He could finally turn his love and loyalty to Muhammadﷺ into effective action. For a long time he had been waiting for such an opportunity. Not so long ago he had had to serve a rich master as a slave. Therefore he had not had the chance to fight together with the other companions. When Salman had left his home country, he had virtually been a boy still. Driven by a deep longing and desire to find answers to all his questions, he had set out to search for God. On his journey he had met Christian saints and had lived with them for a while. From them he learnt that there was to be new messenger soon. But shortly after that he had been taken captive. Muhammadﷺ himself had paid a ransom for him. But not only that: just recently some of the companions, among them Umar, had been boasting about their noble descent. Having named their most important ancestors, they had asked, "And you, Salman, what can you tell us about your origin?"

What was he to say? Under the questioning looks of those present he started to feel more and more uncomfortable. "Some call me the Son of Islam," was all he could think of. At last Muhammadﷺ stepped in for him, saying "He is part of my family." Omar was deeply touched by these words. Ashamed, he said, "None of us should ever ask such inappropriate questions again." "Please excuse our careless talk," the other ones implored him too. "It will not happen again."

Not far away from himself, Salman saw the Prophet's long hair shine in the sun. Muhammad ﷺ, God's chosen Prophet, did not think himself too good to work in the trench together with the others and dig till they dropped. Suddenly a commotion arose at a certain spot in the trench. There was a huge boulder that could not be moved. Without hesitation Salman went over to try his luck. But to no avail! With all his strength he battered the boulder, but the rock did not move an inch and could not be broken to pieces either. At that the Prophet called, "In the name of Allah, the Gracious, the Merciful!" When Muhammad ﷺ himself battered the big rock with these words, it burst. Salman did not believe his eyes. He himself, who was said to have the strength of ten men, had not accomplished what the Prophet had done with one stroke. Three times Muhammad ﷺ let the hoe crash down. In astonishment Salman watched each stroke being accompanied by a flash of lightning. "I can see the roofs of Damascus in Syria," the Prophet said. "Now I can recognise the city of Sanaa in Yemen." At the third stroke he called out, "Before my eyes I can see the white palace of the King of Persia. By Allah, these lands will soon belong to Islam." When Muhammad ﷺ smiled, Salman felt confidence flow through his heart. "We will succeed," he thought, and turned back to his work.

The Siege

A Time of Privation

The trench had just been finished when scouts brought word that Abu Sufyan and his army were already approaching the city from the south. Most of the women together with their children took shelter in their houses, while the warriors positioned themselves. Shortly afterwards the time had come: the silhouettes of the approaching horde of riders appeared at the horizon. The neighing of the horses and the throaty lowing of the camels accompanied the attackers' war songs. Very soon the men of Medina realised just how big this challenge was. Ten thousand men were moving towards the city like a dark mass. The believers caught their breath at this sight. "Oh Allah help us!" they mumbled.

The attackers were approaching single-mindedly when they recognised the Prophet's camp outside the gates of the city. "This way they are going to be easy prey," Abu Sufyan rejoiced, but soon he realised how wrong he was. The entire city was surrounded by a deep trench that was interrupted only by a few boulders or houses. The horses could not get through this trench, and every man who would have tried would have been a living target for the archers on the other side of the trench. Angered by that, Abu Sufyan gave his men the sign to stop and began to confer with the leaders of the other tribes. "To me the only chance seems to be an attack on the city from the other side," one of the men suggested at last. "In this way we can force the Prophet's men to scatter, which would make it easier for us to get through the trench." Huyay from the Banu Nadir interjected: "On the other side of the city there are some Jewish families. They have formed an alliance with Muhammad but do not consider him a prophet. I think that with a little power of persuasion I might succeed in winning them over."

Just a short time later Huyay knocked on the door of Kaab, the representative of the Jews aligned with Muhammad ﷺ. "Let me in, I have to talk to you!" he called. Kaab wanted to refuse at first, but then he yielded to Huyay's urging and let him in. "Listen," Huyay began, "it is better for you to be on our side. Look at our army – you have never seen such an array of tribes before! Muhammad and his handful of men stand no chance of winning this fight. What do you think will happen to your people then? If, on the other hand, Islam is finally defeated, this will result in a lot of benefits for you and your people." In disgust, Kaab wanted to send Huyay out of his house, but when he saw Abu Sufyan's huge army in front of the city, he was terrified and began to feel very scared. He began to doubt whether the decision to stick by Muhammad ﷺ had actually been the right thing. And when eventually Huyay simply tore the alliance document before Kaab's eyes, he just let it happen.

Kaab told his people about Huyay's visit. Although most of them did not believe that Muhammad ﷺ was a prophet, they were not willing to break the alliance. "An agreement has to be adhered to!" they said. "Besides, we are faring well under Muhammad's rule." Yet, after they had seen the multitude of the enemy troops with their own eyes, their resolve began to waver. In the end they yielded to Huyay's urging.

Umar was the first one to become suspicious of the Jews who lived in the southern part of the city. He told the Prophet about a possible betrayal. So Muhammad ﷺ sent out the leaders of some allied tribes to try to make the betrayers turn back to him. At the same time, he sent men into the rear of Medina so as to defend the alleys there against possible intruders.

Several days passed in this way. Huyay's plan did not work out, in spite of all his efforts. Every attempt to cross the trench failed. The siege went on and the morale in the attackers' camp was plummeting. They were hungry and the nights were cold. Besides, the easterly wind had picked up strongly. Sand was whipped across the plains in heavy gusts and entered eyes and nostrils of people and animals. The wind was tugging at the walls of the tents and on their inhabitants' nerves too.

Inside the city food got scarce as well. People in Medina suffered from tension and lack of sleep. They would not be able to endure the siege much longer. Something had to happen.

A man called Nuaym entered the Prophet's camp. He was from the tribe of Ashdja, who were camping in front of the city with Abu Sufyan's troops. He was led to Muhammad ﷺ and told him, "I have come to join you and your people. I believe that you are the Messenger whom God has sent to the people. Your teachings represent the truth. You can order me to do whatever you wish."

"There is something you can do for us," the Prophet replied. "Go and sow the seeds of discord between the tribes who have allied against us. Tell them whatever you like."

Nuaym set out to go to the Jewish quarter first. He was well-known there, so they welcomed him without any suspicion. "Listen," he said to the citizens of the quarter, "I am concerned with your safety. I have to warn you! Our situation does not look very good. Abu Sufyan has not found any way to cross the trench. The horsemen cannot achieve anything and our men are at a loss. Many horses have been injured by arrows and the provisions have been used up. People are suffering from hunger.

If they cannot bring about a breakthrough soon, they will withdraw and go back home. You, however, cannot go home. The Quraysh and the other tribes will leave you at the mercy of Muhammad and his followers and not bother about what will happen to you. You have broken the agreement. To the Muslims you are nothing but betrayers! You are not going to fare very well then." "You are right," those who were listening mumbled with concern. "But what can we do about it?" "Tell them you'll be willing to do something for them if they leave you some of their people as security, so you can make sure they do not just withdraw if their attacks fail," Nuaym whispered slyly. The men promised him to keep silent and not mention Nuaym's name.

A little while later Nuaym returned to the camp of the Quraysh and told them there, "The Jews of the Banu Qurayda tribe have regretted their decision and returned to Muhammad's side. As a proof that they are in earnest this time, they promised him to get some of your noblest men as hostages for him. So when they come to ask you to give them some of your men as a security for your faithfulness, then you know that I have spoken the truth. Do not trust them!"

In order to find out about their allies' state of affairs, Abu Sufyan sent some men to the Banu Qurayda with a message. "We will attack early tomorrow morning," they announced. "Be prepared to fight at our side."

"How do we know that you are not going to abandon us if the attack fails?" they replied. "Give us a few of your men as security so we can be sure that we will all see this matter through together until the end."

Now the besiegers were sure that their new allies had turned away from them again. The scouts returned to their camp furiously to give their report there. All along the Prophet had continued to plead, "Oh Allah, please help us to fend off our enemies! Put them to flight and let them tremble with fear of your power! I ask you to send us your help!"

At nightfall it began to rain. The wind had turned into a tremendous storm driving black shreds of clouds across the night sky. Chillingly cold rain was pelting down on the plains. The storm drove the animals away from each other and tore up the tents. Shivering with cold, the besiegers huddled up, wrapped in blankets and the remains of their tent squares.

Only at daybreak did the storm die down. The men struggled to their feet and scanned the hills with their eyes to find their scattered animals. The impressive army had shrunk to a pathetic group. "This is enough!" Abu Sufyan shouted angrily. "I am going to leave here and I advise all of you to do the same!"

On the other side, in the Prophet's camp, the storm had raged less fiercely, because the tents had been pitched up in a sheltered place beside some buildings and rocks. Yet, the believers were completely exhausted too. Some of them could hardly remember when they had last slept a few hours in a row or had some food. Aisha, Umm Salamah and Zaynab had also insisted to remain a few days and nights in Muhammad's tent.

They all rose stumbling unsteadily when Bilal called for Morning Prayer.

When after a little while the companions were told by Muhammad ﷺ that the enemy's army had withdrawn they could hardly believe their good fortune. Radiant with joy they went home and thanked Allah for their wondrous salvation.

Among the Banu Qurayda there were only a few people who wanted to join Islam after the defeat. The others, hoping for a milder sentence, asked the Prophet for permission to be judged by a man from their own tribe, and they affirmed that they would accept this judgement. Abu Saad, a follower of the Prophet's from the Qurayda tribe, was approved by everyone to be the judge. However, Abu Saad was by no means mild-mannered. He had seen the Banu Nadir rise up against the Prophet a second time. During the siege, when he had accompanied Umar to the negotiation talks, he had been witness of the perfidious betrayal.

Abu Saad had been severely injured himself, and he already sensed that he would soon be leaving this world. How was he to leave the Prophet behind amidst those traitors? Knowing Muhammad ﷺ well, he was sure that he would show leniency yet again.

"My verdict is that the culprits be killed and the women and children be taken captives," he decreed.

This verdict was in keeping with the sentence for treason in Jewish law, and it was implemented soon afterwards.

Umm Salamah

Hope for Peace

Umm Salamah's litter was swaying along gently; the leisurely pace of the camel below her made her feel sleepy. Yet Umm Salamah was well aware of the fact that this journey was going to be anything but a pleasure trip. Outside the seclusion of her litter were the men who had gathered, willing to once again fight the Meccans together with the Prophet. This army was getting bigger by the minute. The Prophet had decided to conquer the city of Mecca once and for all, thus putting an end to war. Besides, he wanted to make the Holy Kaaba accessible for all believers again. Umm Salamah had the honour to accompany the Prophet on this expedition. Only recently had she moved into the Prophet's house. Her husband had been killed in one of the many conflicts with the Prophet's enemies. She had been left behind alone with four children. "I will take care of you and your children," Muhammad ﷺ had assured her. Umm Salamah knew several women whose husbands had also fallen in battle. The Prophet himself as well as his companions tried to take these destitute women and their children into their own families and to provide for them. Quarrels and jealousy came about, to be sure, but nevertheless Umm Salamah was happy to be part of the Prophet's household.

The horrible defeat at Uhud had claimed the greatest number of victims. Umm Salamah could not forget how Hind, drenched in hate, had been singing songs of joy next to Hamzah's dead body.

All the more she found it remarkable how leniently the Prophet treated his own captives. When someone was willing to cease their hatred and to repent, then they were forgiven. Some of the captives were so impressed by this generosity that they began to ardently admire their former enemy.

The same was true for Khalid, the man who had commanded the enemy's cavalry in the battle of Uhud. Meanwhile he and many of his horsemen had adopted Islam and fought on the Prophet's side. One day Khalid's men came out as winners from a battle against an enemy tribe. When the captives had been disarmed, they agreed to adopt Islam as well. However, Khalid mistrusted their intentions. He considered them hypocrites, and so he killed the men. When the Prophet heard about this deed he began to weep. "Oh my God," he cried, "up to this moment I was innocent, I was innocent up to this deed!" Finally he sent Ali to the killed men's families. He was to make every effort to amend at least part of this guilt. Ali went up to the families and talked to them. In the end he paid them a large amount of gold as blood money.

Later the Prophet said to Khalid, "Our religion forbids us to punish those who have converted from evil to good. Should not a Muslim be someone from whose hand and tongue everybody is safe? We have not been ordered to abolish humanity — we have the task to reintroduce it! Oh Khalid, you will have to answer to Allah for this deed!" Dismayed at these harsh words, Khalid replied, "My Prophet, these men's words did not come from their hearts!" At that the Prophet answered, "Have you opened their hearts and looked into them? Only Allah knows what really goes on in a person's heart."

In the past few years there had been fights between the two parties over and over again. However, the Quraysh could no longer prevent Islam from spreading. Fear was growing in the Meccans, fear of the increasing number of their adversaries. For this reason, they had even made a peace agreement with the Muslims some time ago. Sadly, the Quraysh did not abide by it for long. In spite of the agreement they attacked time and time again.

Now Muhammad ﷺ was on his way to Mecca with around twenty thousand men. Never before had any leader succeeded in uniting so many Arabic tribes for a cause. The Quraysh would not be able to accomplish anything against such an army.

The men were seized by eager excitement. Surrounded by the voices and sounds of people and camels around her, Umm Salama was swaying along in her litter. "Oh Allah," she whispered, "let there be peace soon."

Return to Mecca

Day of Mercy

Muhammad's troops were camping a short distance from Mecca. Word had got about in the whole valley that Muhammad ﷺ had come with a huge army in order to capture the city. Fear was spreading among the citizens of Mecca. For so many years, the Meccans had persecuted and tormented the believers. "How are they going to punish us for that if Muhammad ﷺ manages to capture our city?" they were wondering gloomily.

Muhammad's uncle Abbas also lived in Mecca. In secret he had long sided with the Muslims. Also, he had been the one who had informed the Prophet about the Meccans' plans before the battle of Uhud. To be able to live in Mecca still, he had kept his views a secret. Now he decided that the time had come for him to publicly confess to Islam. Having done this he advised Abu Sufyan to do the same: "It is your only chance to escape with your life!" Reluctantly, Abu Sufyan let Abbas lead him into the Prophet's camp. Immediately Umar got sight of the man who had fought his beloved Prophet for so many years. Umar would have loved nothing better than to kill him right away, but Muhammad ﷺ prevented him from doing it with just a few words. Abu Sufyan had come to deliver his confession of faith in front of Muhammad ﷺ. "La ilaha illallah, I bear witness that there is only one God," he said hesitantly. Of course the Prophet noticed that these words were not spoken with conviction, but he wanted to give Abu Sufyan the time he needed. Abu Sufyan had done so many horrible things to the Muslims over the years that he was now deeply impressed by the Prophet's generosity. When the talk was over, Abbas led him to a place from where they could watch the Prophet's men. There they were all gathered, the tribes of the desert: the Ansar, the Khuza'a, the Muzayna, the Juhayna, the Ashja and countless others. At this moment, Abu Sufyan finally realised that the Meccans' fight against the Prophet and his religion was lost.

Upon Abu Sufyan's return to Mecca he told his people, "Muhammad will take this city. Nothing can stop him. Go into your houses and lock the doors."

When shortly afterwards the Prophet and his men rode into the city, they met no resistance.

On his arrival, Muhammad ﷺ first turned to the citizens of Mecca, who were hiding behind their doors and windows, listening in fright. "Oh you people of Quraysh! What do you think I am going to do to you?" he called. "Only good things," they replied cautiously, "for you are the son of one of our noblest brothers." "You are all free!" the

Prophet announced at that. "Do not be afraid. Not one of you will be harmed. This is the day of mercy!"

Accompanied by his companions' shouts of joy, he rode to the Kaaba. Together with Ali he entered the holy house. "The moment of truth has come," Muhammad ﷺ said, "and there is an end to falsehood now, just as everything that is not true will end one day." Muhammad ﷺ and Ali removed all the idols and statues from the holy house and destroyed them. Then the Prophet walked around the Kaaba seven times and drank from the holy water from the Zamzam well.

Joyfully the other Muslims also came streaming to the Kaaba now. At last they could approach the holy house again to pray there and drink water from the holy well. After a short while Ali came and brought the key to the Kaaba to Muhammad ﷺ, asking him, "Please assign to our family the service at the Kaaba, and allow us to give the water to the pilgrims!" The Prophet took the key but sent for Uthman ibn Talha. "Today is also a day of kindness and faithfulness, Uthman!" Muhammad ﷺ said smiling. "Here is your key."

A little later, not far from the hill of Safa, the Prophet received those who up to that day had been his enemies and who now came to adopt Islam. Men and women came to him in hundreds. One of the women was particularly heavily veiled. She was afraid of being recognised by the Prophet's followers before having the chance to talk to Muhammad ﷺ. When she was finally standing in front of him, she greeted him saying, "Messenger of God, Allah be praised. He let you and your religion prevail!" Then she declared, "I therefore have

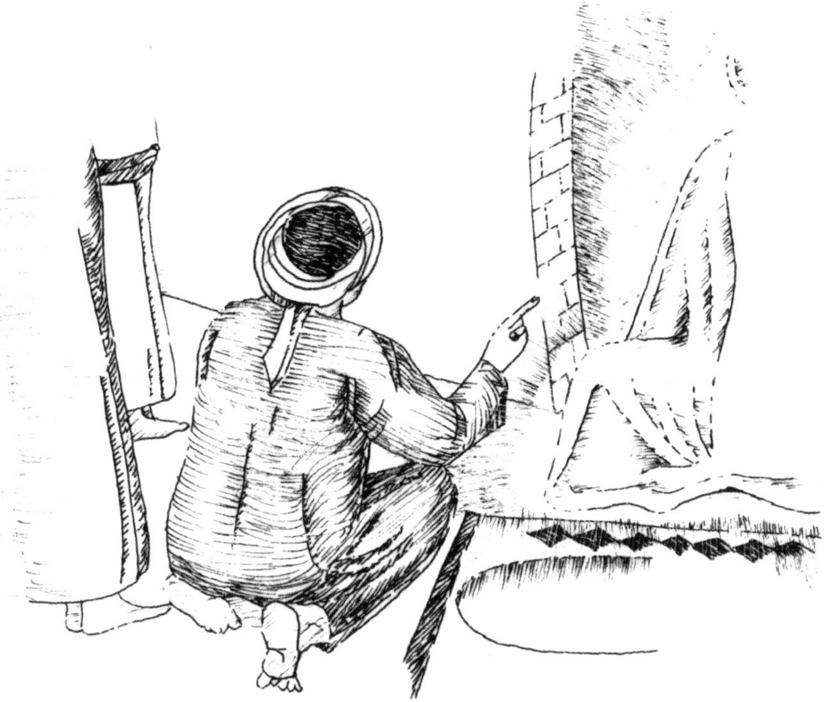

adopted your faith, too." With these words she lifted her veil. "I am Hind, the daughter of Utbah." "Welcome!" the Prophet replied.

Many people were so impressed by the Prophet's compassion and generosity that they also agreed to acknowledge Muhammad ﷺ as their leader and as the Messenger of God.

The Prophet's companions watched him give presents to some of the new Muslims. Now those companions who were from Medina began to be afraid that the Prophet might intend to stay in Mecca from now on. When Muhammad ﷺ heard this, he gathered them around him and told them, "They only take a few presents home, whereas you can take the Messenger of God with you. Are you not satisfied with this?" The Medinans were very glad when they realised what Muhammad ﷺ meant by that.

The Prophet stayed in Mecca for fifteen nights, and then he set out for Medina again. When he saw the shape of his city from the distance, he was so pleased that he began to cheer, "There is no deity but God! The Earth and everything that exists belongs to Him, and He has the power over all things!"

The Farewell

Fatima's Secret

Muhammad ﷺ had become the ruler over all the tribes of Arabia by now. He could therefore have indulged himself in all sorts of luxury, but the Prophet did not have any interest in riches except where he could give them away to others. He considered himself no more than a servant of Allah. Therefore he preferred to keep living a very modest life. The furnishing of his room consisted of a simple sleeping mat and a sheepskin on the wall. The few clothes and shoes he needed he made with his own hands. Also, he provided for his family himself, taking care of them as he had always done. He treated all the people he encountered in a loving and caring manner.

As was his habit he never went to sleep until he had given his last dinar to the poor. Sometimes he even went hungry since there often was someone near who urgently needed food, and so the Prophet simply passed on his portion. To his wife Aisha he once said, "Aisha, never send a beggar away with empty hands!"

One day, Muhammad ﷺ received a coat as a present. A while later a man came who was feeling cold, and at once the Prophet gave him the coat.

Muhammad ﷺ continued to spend a great part of his time teaching people about religious issues. In most cases he gave people simple answers. These words of advice, however, were quite challenging and not always easy to follow. Once, for instance, he was asked, "Honoured Prophet, please tell me: what are the most important things I have to be mindful of as a Muslim?"

The Prophet declared, "Believe in Allah and never speak ill of another person."

In the tenth year following the emigration, the Prophet and his family went on the pilgrimage to Mecca once again. After going around the holy Kaaba seven times, he went down to the plains of Arafat. There he climbed on a hill and began to speak to the people:

"Listen carefully to what I tell you; for I do not know if I will return to this place another time. Do not forget that one day you will face your God. Allah will ask you about your deeds. Then you will have to bear responsibility for everything you did in your life. Do not forget that you are brothers and sisters. Do not hinder the Jews and Christians who want to retain their faith in their religion. Do not betray each other and do not act unjustly. Never take anything from someone else unless it is given to you willingly. Be kind with your wives and take good care of those entrusted to you. I am leaving you a clear guideline – the Holy Quran that contains the word of God, and in addition to that everything I taught you. If you act according to it, you will not go astray. Listen to my words and comprehend! Allah is my witness that I have brought to you the message of Islam."

A few days after his speech, Muhammad ﷺ was visited by Jibril again. "Allah the Almighty is sending me to you with a message. He leaves it to you to decide," the Angel said. "If you wish to, you may lead a long life in this world. After that, Paradise is open to you. But you can also decide to return now to Allah the Almighty, our merciful Creator."

Even though the angel had left the choice to him, the Prophet realised that Allah wanted to call him to come.

"I have already made up my mind," the Prophet replied, "I want to go to my Lord!"

Soon afterwards Muhammad ﷺ fell ill. His head was resting in Aisha's lap most of the time or leaning against her chest. But when Fatima came to visit her father, Aisha withdrew from the room as she did not want to disturb the two. One time, however, Aisha watched Muhammad ﷺ whisper something to his daughter, at which Fatima began to weep. Then the Prophet whispered something to her again, at which she smiled.

"Are you going to tell me what you were talking about?" Aisha asked her a little later. "It's a secret," Fatima smiled. "I would rather keep it to myself."

Not long after that, however, she told Aisha about it: "He told me that he was going to die from this disease," she whispered. "I started to cry. Then he told me that I would be the first one from our family to follow him to the hereafter, and so I smiled."

Many people came to Muhammad's house to visit the diseased man. They all were distressed when they realised the condition he was in.

"Do not be sad," the Prophet told his companions, "we will see each other quite soon. I will be waiting for you at the bridge to Paradise, where I will ask Allah to lead each one of you over safely."

A few days later, Muhammad ﷺ died in Aisha's arms.

At this time, prophets were buried at the place they had died. So with the help of Abu Bakr, Ali and some others, Muhammad's body was laid to rest in the ground of Aisha's room.

"This world and I are like a tree and a rider," the Prophet had once told Aisha. "The rider just takes a short rest in the tree's shade before moving on."

And so Muhammad's soul set forth on the journey to the highest heaven, as Allah had promised him.

Chronological Table

Approximate year according to the Christian calendar

570	Prophet Muhammad ﷺ is born in Mecca
576	His mother Amina dies
578	His grandfather Abdul Muttalib dies
595	Wedding with Khadijah
610	First Revelation in the cave of Hira
621	Night Journey on the Buraq
622	Emigration from Mecca to Medina
624	Battle at the wells of Badr
625	Defeat at Uhud
627	Battle of the Trench
630	Conquest of Mecca
632	Last pilgrimage and farewell address at Arafat Muhammad ﷺ dies in Aisha's arms

Mediterranean Sea
Syria
Bos
Jerus
Egypt
Red Sea
Abyssi